IT REALLY HAPPENED
HERE & THERE!

MORE ROUND TABLES TALES
FROM ETHELYN PEARSON

Ethelyn Pearson

IT REALLY HAPPENED HERE & THERE!
MORE ROUND TABLE TALES FROM ETHELYN PEARSON

Author - Ethelyn Pearson
Publisher - McCleery & Sons Publishing

International Standard Book Number: 1-931916-37-3
Printed in the United States of America.

ACKNOWLEDGMENTS

Dozens of cooperative resources made the gathering of information found in this book possible. It is with trepidation that I make this list, fearful of leaving out some valuable contributing source. Stories came via old books, ledgers, newspapers, by mouth from generous people who share memories, and micro film found in the archives of The Hewitt Historical Society Museum, East Otter Tail Museum, Wadena County Historical Museum, Todd County Museum, Stevens County Historical Society, Clay County Historical Society, Bertha Historical Museum, Alexandria Historical Museum, County Museum in Park Rapids, Stearns County Historical Society, and Sam Brown Historical Center in Brown's Valley, South Dakota. Newspapers who proved to be useful were Staples World, Wadena Pioneer Journal, Long Prairie Leader, Independent Herald in Clarissa, Sauk Centre Herald, The Fargo Forum, The Morris Tribune, Fergus Falls Daily, Brainerd Dispatch, St. Cloud Times, Verndale Sun, and Prime Time in Detroit Lakes. I did research in city libraries in Wadena, Staples, New York Mills, Park Rapids, Moorhead State University, Minnesota State University in St. Paul, and Brainerd.

Having always been a collector of old history books, I used Indian Hunts and Indian Hunters Of The Old West, Warren's History Of The Ojibawa Nation, Northern Lights, The Story Of Minnesota's Past, Men To Remember, The Last Full Measure, Dusty Trails and Iron Rails, Dakota Portraits, Representative Americans, First Person America, Great Western Indian Fights, The Year Of The Century, The Valley Of Shadows, Age Of Great Depression, The Oregon Trail, Gem Of The Prairie, Tales They Told, Compton Township History, Ten Years A Cowboy, White Rock, Unsung Heroes, Investor's Syndicate, The Last Of The Tearoom Ladies, McNair, The Famous and Almost Famous, The Wheat Trail, 101 Stories of Minnesota, Old Rail Fences, Sod House Days, Trapper Days, plus others.

Sincere gratitude to special friends who shared their stories and material in the way of pictures and reports. They are Pastor Vern Burgeson, Robert Zosel, Carrie Lindblom, and Administrator Michael Gibson of Fair Oaks Lodge for letting me take time in a work day to record the stories of residents whose interesting lives lend to enhance the flavor of "Round Table Tales."

Ethelyn Pearson

—

DEDICATION

In loving memory of a great mom, Alice Linnell Young, who treasured everything I wrote and saved them all, and of a husband, Milton Pearson, who shared an interest in history with me. Also, to my children, Larry (and Pat), Arlen (and Norma), and Linda (and Don, deceased) Bokinskie.

Most of all to my great-grandchildren wherein lies my single claim to the future. They are Andrew, Zachary, Taylor, Matthew, Rebecca, Sarah, Brandon, Baileigh and Kalea, along with little angels Blake and Jordan. My hope is that these brief flashes into the past and the brave souls who lived them will somehow juggle into providing a pattern of continuity that Shakespeare called "the whirligigs of time."

How comforting to know that the same God who guided the footsteps of my great-grandparents is still there for my great-grandchildren and beyond.

—

TABLE OF CONTENTS

"Dear Brother"

An Actual Pioneer Diary from this Region!

ANSON NORTHRUP

My Dear Brother
January 16, 1856

Your letter of the 26th is at hand. I note what you say about the source of Mississippi River. The historical Society has that information. I left Grand Portage on the North Shore of Lake Superior, now the boundary line between the United States and British Possessions in July of 1802, and arrived at Leech Lake in September the same year. On October 1st I went and wintered on the head waters of one of the branches of Crow Wing River, Shell Lake.

Our Indians were Pillagers. In the winter of 1803-1804, I went and wintered at Wild Rice Lake. I passed by Red Cedar Lake, now called "Cass Lake" and followed the Mississippi to Cross Lake, and then up the Mississippi to Elk Lake, now called "Itasca Lake," the source of the great Mississippi River. A short distance this side I made a portage to get to Rice River. I discovered no trace of any white man before me, for I was the first that saw and examined the shores. Shell River is an ideal place for a trading post, there being a beautiful location on Section 11, which was undoubtable the place where Morisson's Trading Post was located in October of 1802.

The first settlers in the county of Shell Lake in recent years were the families of Doran and Henry Smith. Doran took a homestead and built a house on the southeast quarter of the same section. Angeline Kenny married Joseph Brewer in 1872. When she went to Green Valley township to live with her new husband the quarter she had settled on was taken by Frank Wilson, who came in the fall of 1881. Only three people lived in Shell Lake township for three years. The next neighbors north were 15 miles away.

Indians made constant demands that the settlers move as they claimed land as far north as Shell Lake. Young braves threatened to kill both families. An encampment of 30 lodges were only a half-mile away. Indians threw knives at the Dorans while they were building their log house.

The first road was established, but Norman Kittsen claims he used the trail in the early thirties. The Anson Northrup trip with machinery for the old North Star Steamboat passed over the same route. The North Star was dismantled at the mouth of Gull River on the Mississippi and hauled by piece on sleds to the Red River. Northrup left St. Paul on February 26, 1869, and arrived in Sauk Rapids on the 28th with a span of horses and wagon. There was no snow on the ground.

Northrup was told he could go no farther than Platt River with a wagon. He bought a light sled and loaded my wagon on it. They stopped at Luther's, about half way between Platt River and Swan River that night, the wagon was left there and they loaded the truck on a sled and made Crow Wing the following night. They arrived at Otter Tail City the following night, the 5th of March, and found a part of the Northrup expedition. Another part had gone

ahead to build a bridge across the Otter Tail River at an upper crossing that was not frozen over. The snow was deep. Sixteen or more feet!

A flour mill was set up on Bass Creek where it flows out of Long Prairie, at the northwest edge of Hubbard. (The flour mill on the Wing River was built and operated by the Britz Brothers to take care of some wheat that comes in by trade. Fire took the mill in 1900. The elevator at Verndale was erected by Mose Stewart in about 1911, and a couple of years later it was sold to Bert Petit and his brother - *the author*.) Are you getting tired of Shell River news and about elevators? It is the big topic here, and not much other news, I am afraid.

Did you know Jake Graba? His halfway house was a blessing. Logs 100 feet long went into the making of his stable, with stalls on both sides. Much of the time it is full. The driver could sleep inside the house. Well, dear brother, I hope this finds you as healthy and happy as I am, a condition that can change in the twinkle of an eye on this lonesome frontier.

I remain your brother,
James

Mystery of the Headless Hermit

The body of Jimmy McQuat, minus his head and arms, was found on June 27, 1919, by forest ranger T.C. Campbell. McQuat had disappeared nearly a year before from his White Otter Lake castle.

While still a boy, Jimmy was mistaken for someone else by a stranger with mystic powers who predicted that Jimmy would not die in a shack. After several ventures failed, McQuat headed for anonymity in the deep woodland of the north. He discouraged any curious person who happened by, other than lumbermen and prospectors who seemed to like him.

Jimmy made sure that he would not die in a shack by building himself a veritable castle, 34 x 24 feet and three stories high with a tower! It was built entirely of logs. He shaped himself on his acreage on the lake north of Savanna. His castle was finished inside and made very livable. A garden surrounded the house, most unusual in deep timber this far north.

It is hard for those few who knew Jimmy to believe he fell in White Otter Lake and became entangled in fish nets. He was an accomplished swimmer and especially careful. Whether the stranger's prediction when he was a child was fact or fiction, Jimmy took no chance his end would come in a shack. Today, he lies buried in the tomb he made for himself. Where his head and arms ended up is anyone's guess.

White Otter Castle, home of the famous Headless Hermit, whose dismemberment remains a spooky legend.

The Night Cry!
How Grieving German Immigrants Survived by Their Wits in the New World

After their son William died, Oscar and Hilma decided to join friends in America who said it was easier to make a living here. William had died of a malady known as "the night cry." Babies who fell victim began crying at sunset and screamed until sunrise. No matter what the parents tried this pattern was repeated night after night by babies until they died, leaving an exhausted family.

When all the arrangements had been made Oscar and Hilma, with their only surviving son, Herman, traveled to Exonica, Wisconsin, where Hilma had relatives. Their family grew to eight children. Hilma took in washing and made woven rugs on a hand-made loom. Oscar ran a hand-car to inspect tracks after each train. In 1805, they moved to Minnesota. Here, their building caught fire and they had a narrow escape. They joined a German community about forty miles away.

During these years Hilma had to use all of her skills to keep her family healthy. She was also the community mid-wife. The children were taught to recognize the leaves and berries of plants with various medicinal qualities. Camomile tea was a standby. Sumach, when processed, did quite well for a cough. Horehound boiled with sugar made effective cough drops. Peppermint settled an upset stomach, and catnip leaves worked for a bellyache. Honey spread over a burn held down the pain, keeping out air and infection. Plantain leaves couldn't be beat when applied to an infected sore. Smut, the black fungus that grows on corn stalks, contained ergot to stop hemorrhaging.

There were ways to keep food safe the year round. Hilma made use of them all. Fresh meat was fried in deep grease until barely done, then placed in stone crocks with the grease an inch deep on top to seal the meat. Pork, beef, and goose meat were ground, made into balls and fried a bit, then put down in grease. The grease made a favorite flavored sandwich spread for Oscar and the boys when they went to cut wood.

Every family had a smoke house in which hams, bacon, or whole hogs were cured. Sausage, head cheese, and liver sausage were made and stored in a cool cellar. Corn was cut from the cob, spread in flat pans, covered with a cloth, and put on the porch roof to dry out of harms way. It had to be stirred often and it took several sunny days to dry. It was then kept in a sugar sack hung from the ceiling in a spare room.

The children's favorite were choke cherries, June berries, and plums dried the same way. During the long winter, these were set out in dishes for the children to eat at will, like candy but much healthier. Children were expected to help in some way: picking something for the table, knitting, scrubbing floors, washing milk separators, driving horses, stacking grain, cleaning the barn, or herding cows. Children were taught to work as soon as they could do something. A favorite job was herding cows. Then they could play with neighbor kids herding cows in an adjoining meadow. Feltman (field man), their dog, was so intelligent he could almost take care of the cows by himself.

By using everything available to her to keep her family healthy, Hilma managed to raise her big family. They were never sorry they came to America. In Germany, a share of what was grown was given to the land owner. In America, they could keep what they worked for.

"We're Republicans, Don't Shoot!"
Wacky Ship Nearly Killed the President

On November 14, 1943, a torpedo was sent scorching its way across the cold Atlantic, aimed at Battleship Iowa, the ship President Roosevelt and Secretary of State Cordell Hull had boarded, with top military brass, on their way to Teheran for the conference with Stalin and Churchill. While we slept, world history for all of us could have changed at the batting of an eye. This bit of history was soft pedaled, kept under wraps, buried under a pile of mundane reports somewhere in Miami until a reporter, looking for something else, found the story, bringing it to the attention of the public almost 50 years later.

The war was at its hottest. The route the Iowa, with its precious load, had to take cut directly across what was known to be a German U-boat feeding ground. The Iowa was under wartime orders, meaning there was to be no noise, no radio contact, no lights. All the Iowa had as a defense was speed and silence. Two destroyers accompanied her, as well as a new ship which had just slid into the waves for the first time. Commissioned July 19, 1943, the William D. Porter, was commanded by Wilfred Walker. The crew, while untried, was proud to be among the escort ships chosen to be in so important a convoy.

The night before they left Norfolk on their way to North Africa. The Porter, called "The Willie D," came too close and backed out the length of a sister ship, the Luce, tearing out her anchor, and knocking down railings, life rafts, the ship's boat, and other more valuable items. The Willie D. only suffered a scratched anchor. This was only the beginning of Willie D's destructive future.

Twenty-four hours later the convoy was in motion, with strict orders not to use the radios under any conditions. The dense blacked-out night suddenly exploded with a tremendous roar and bright flashes of fire that frightened the entire convoy. Reluctantly, Captain Walker had to admit that one of the Willy D's depth charges had not been adequately secured and had rolled off the back of his ship.

The next morning a huge rogue wave washed over the Willie D, taking everything unsecured. One sailor was washed away and could not be found. Next, the fire room lost power in one of the boilers. This would, in retrospect, have been the time any prudent individual would have turned tail and run for port. Instead, Walker and his green crew struggled on. Among other vessels, it had already gained the reputation of being a bad luck ship.

The weather on the morning of November 14 was fair with a moderate sea roll. President Roosevelt and Hull were anxious to see exactly how a ship under fire could defend herself, so the captain of the Iowa staged a sporadic session with real live ammunition. The captain of the Iowa wanted to prove in front of this prestigious audience that Iowa was truly "Monarch of the Seas." She put up a number of weather balloons to be shot at in practice.

On the Willie D, Captain Walker was envious of those on the Iowa, so he sent his crew to battle stations to shoot at the balloons the Iowa gunners missed. Impatiently, the gunners waited for their turn to show this president how good they were. Down in the torpedo room, Tony Fazio and Lawton Dawson were responsible for the torpedoes. Part of their job was to see that the primers were attached to the torpedoes during practice and to remove them as soon as it was over. Dawson went about his tasks, forgetting that he had not replaced one of the primers. A new torpedo officer up on the bridge, unaware of the danger, ordered what he thought was only a simulated firing.

Lt. Steward Lewis, standing on the bridge, saw the torpedo hit the water on its way to the Iowa and its valuable cargo 6000 rods away. Innocently, he asked Walker, "Did you give permission to fire a live torpedo?"

Captain Walkers reply is hardly fit to print. Being in German sub country, he was reluctant to use the radio to warn the Iowa. Then reality sank in. The flagship had to be warned. A warning light was flashed. Then the Willie D flashed they were going to reverse. Throwing caution to the wind, the Willie D signaled Lion, the Iowa's code name: "Turn right!"

After what seemed an eternity, she did come around.

On Iowa's bridge, word of the wild torpedo had reached Roosevelt. He asked that his chair be moved up to the rail so he could see what was going to likely kill him. One of the secret service men drew his pistol. Was he going to kill that thing? A few minutes later there was a terrible, terrible explosion just behind the Iowa. Speeding up had kicked up enough of a back wash to set off the torpedo.

The Willie D fell under suspicion. Was it in an assassination plot? The Iowa trained her guns on the Willie D. The immediate crisis was over, and so was Captain Walter's career. The last thing he had to say to the Iowa was a faint, "We did it." Very shortly the new ship and its green crew were arrested and told to go to Bermuda to be tried. Never before had a ship's entire company been arrested. They were surrounded by marines with weapons drawn when they docked.

Torpedo man Dawson finally admitted that he left the primer on the torpedo tube. He also threw the used tube over the side to cover his mistake. Walker and several others found themselves in boring jobs ashore, and Dawson was sentenced to 14 years of hard labor. President Roosevelt contended that it was an accident, pure and simple, and no one should be punished. The destroyer Willie D was stationed up near the Aleutians where she could do no more harm. She was there several years, then was reassigned to the Western Pacific. Before she left, she sent a five-inch shell by mistake into the front yard of an American base commandant, ruining a fancy flower bed. She distinguished herself by shooting down a number of Japanese aircraft, until it was revealed there were American planes among them. Sadly, this often happened when ships shot at planes.

Finally in April of 1947, the Willie D was sent to Okinawa. The greetings from other ships whenever the Willie D hove into sight, was "We're Republicans, Don't Shoot!" Her sister ship, the USS Luce, was not so nice when, again by accident, the Willie D riddled her side and superstructure with gunfire. On June 10, 1947, the William D. Porter's luck ran out. She was sunk by a plane which had "attacked" under water! The plane was made almost all of wood, so it didn't set off detector devices in the harbor and did not register on radar.

A kamikaze pilot headed for the Willie D had missed when the Willie D pulled to one side and had instead hit another destroyer. There was a big sigh of relief, then a monstrous explosion under the Willie D. The Japanese plane had slid over and blown up.

Hours later, the last man on board of the doomed Willie D was the captain. The ship that almost changed world history in the blink of an eyelash, slipped quietly into 2,400 feet of water to wait out eternity. For her there would be no more mistakes.

It almost seemed that she intended to let her crew off before joining history.

Taking the crew off of the sinking USS William D. Porter, June 10, 1945.

Whoa! Dumit, I said Whoa!
Pioneer Postman is Chased by Tin Lizzie

William Beck hurried Bird and Nellie along with a flip of the reins on their broad behinds. He would be glad when this week was over. Catalog time, the bane of every mailman. They were bulky, heavy, and would not fit in most mail boxes. There would be Montgomery Ward, then Spiegel after the first batches of Sears Roebuck. All the seeds catalogs were next but didn't weigh so much.

Will was one of Hewitt, Minnesota's, earliest mail carriers. He was considered knowledgeable because he taught school a few years before he heard of the mail carrier job and got it. The first thing he did was make a comfortable cab, with a soft high chair, and a little stove for those cold days. People could see him coming from a ways off by the smoke from his stove. Often, there would be somebody wanting something or wanting just to say hello to the mailman. He sold stamps, money orders, and gave those who needed a ride into town a lift. Sometimes they sent a can of cream or a crate of eggs to be dropped off at the creamery. Will always claimed that he couldn't think of a single time anyone had taken advantage of him because of his agreeable nature. Like other mailmen of that day, Will obliged when he could.

Delivering reams of information about each family without snooping a single post card was natural, but he was likely aware that one of his family's sons seldom wrote home. He hated most of all delivering those letters from everybody's relative in Washington, Uncle Sam, with the notice that they had been "chosen" to serve in the army. He usually had a cake or loaf of fresh bread from his wife, Winona, often called "Nona," to be left off there on his next trip. If a death occurred, he stopped by a few minutes to give what comfort and condolence he could.

Most of the time, Will enjoyed his job very much, not withstanding the fact he hated several dogs on his route, who waited without fail to chase his team. One time, the horses gave a jump that upset

Winona Beck

the stove, setting the cab on fire. It turned out not too badly, with no mail burned and only Will's pants leg singed stamping out the fire.

In those days, if there had been a modern way of getting a bad weather report out, it would not have made any difference. The U.S. Mail went through, delivering almost everything from wedding rings to horse harnesses.

Finally, when Will retired after a number of years, it was his unfailing service, so willingly given, that was most apt to be recalled. Still, folks laughed themselves sick over his first experiences with a Model T Ford after Bird and Nellie retired. Like the Fords of the era, she was named "Lizzie." Before he learned where the brake was he yelled, "Whoa!" a few times.

At home, Will parked the car on a hill. Proudly, he gave the shiny new crank a healthy whirl. She popped right into action on the first try and immediately started toward him. Will tried running backward so that he could get out of her way and climb aboard. It didn't take long to see that Lizzie was gaining on him. In one giant leap, Will cleared the bumper and landed astraddle the radiator.

Lizzie picked up speed while Will frantically waved his straw hat, yelling "Whoa!" one more time,

then just concentrated on hanging on. The commotion set the dog to barking wildly and Nona came to the stoop just in time to see Lizzie, with Will still aboard, run smack into her hen house. Boards, shingles, feathers, half-naked chickens, and one straw hat flew in all directions. A fair sprinkling of chickens remained on the site, never to cackle again.

Lizzie came to a stop at last on a level place with Will a bit green but still hanging on, looking through the windshield from the wrong direction. He was almost sorry when it stopped, he said later,

because now he had to deal with Nona. Standing arms akimbo in outrage, she announced, "And now, Mr. Will Beck, you can just go to work and build me a new hen house! I declare, never saw anything like it. And at your age!"

In due time, the hen house was rebuilt, Will learned to drive and after several years of retirement died of a heart attack.

Winona lived to be a very sprightly, alert 104!

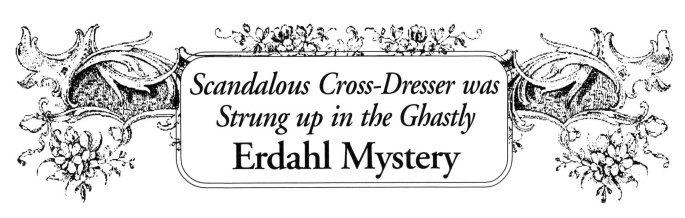

Scandalous Cross-Dresser was Strung up in the Ghastly Erdahl Mystery

A long time ago, in this very region, a man's body was found in a thicket of Plum trees, a half mile from the road. A small rope was tied around the man's neck with a slip knot. The limb the rope was tied to was only about an inch thick, allowing the man's knees to touch the ground. Death could have come about by strangulation, but the small tree was bent over, which seems to prove it was not a suicide. Why not choose a longer rope and a bigger tree if you're seriously trying to shed the woes of this old world?

While definitely a man, the body was dressed neatly in no less than three corsets and other feminine garments. All the buttons were buttoned, and the bosom was padded to resemble breasts, a get-up that must have taken hours of preparation. All of this and a full beard! Clumsy work shoes were the only male attire.

One thing is certain. The man could not have dressed like this in public without attracting attention. When the rope was removed, the body retained its kneeling position. Men's socks, some socks sewn together, thread and scissors, a map of Kansas, printed material including several almanacs and a few other articles were in a neat pile under the plum tree. Only the map of Kansas seemed to be a clue. If this was a case of murder, the culprit could have arranged the pile.

This was the second mysterious case. On July 11 of that year, a corpse was found on the A.K. Lee farm not over a mile away. There is no doubt this was murder, also a mystery. Some thought he might have been a peddler robbed of his wares.

In any event, the real story of each of these murders may never be known.

Herman Haunts Sauk Centre

When a young carpenter called Herman showed up three miles west of Sauk Centre in September 1928, one can surmise he received a less than friendly welcome, since he was smeared over 60 feet of railroad track and five trains have passed over him. The body had been dragged down the track 50 feet.

Herman's address book identified relatives. A brother recognized a lapel pin and picture. No money. He was eulogized as a person with no foul traits, one who made no enemies. He called men acquaintances, friends. Later, the *St. Cloud Times* printed a story that claimed five men of the Great Northern Railroad had sighted the ghost of Herman, silently walking the tracks. The *Journal Press*, reminding people several trains had run over Herman, wrote, "In the dusk of the fall of the evening the man's wraith may be seen walking steadily down the railroad track, until he comes to the place he was found dead, and then it suddenly vanishes into nothingness."

A copy of the story even found its way to the Census Department in Washington, DC, where a young woman employee named Minnesota Madison read the tale. She was the daughter of Mr. and Mrs. J. Madison of Osakis.

Miss Madison was attracted to what she called "psyclyre phenomena." After reading the account of the ghost she sent a letter to her acquaintance Lewis H. Vath, principal of the St. Cloud-Sauk Center business colleges. Miss Madison, upon meditation, came to the conclusion that Herman's spirit was returning because he wanted to relate something to the living. Her letter became the topic of conversation in Osakis.

The *St. Cloud Times* and *Sauk Centre Herald* heaped ridicule on *St. Cloud Journal Press* for printing anything to do with ghosts. In defense, the *Journal* printed the following: "Section Foreman Fiala states that he and his crew and the following crew have all seen the ghost. They have seen a hatless man dressed like Herman was when he was found on the railroad tracks, always walking up and down, up and down. They have called to him but every time they get close he vanishes.

"One time they planned to come from one direction while the section crew came from the other direction, trapping the ghost between them. When they did this and got too close the ghost disappeared into thin air. When the section men found the body they cut a swatch from his coat for the purposes of identification, when they finally saw him he was shy of that garment. Two detectives sent out from Minneapolis saw the ghost but were unable to arrest it. Fiala says he is not afraid to take on anyone, night or day. Since he never harmed poor Herman, he is not afraid of its vengeance. At least 200 persons have seen the ghost to date."

Despite the fact that Herman was from Evansville, the *Evansville Enterprise* wouldn't mention any of the ghostly action unless the editor had positive proof of the ghost. A citizen from Evansville wrote to a friend in Sauk Centre to ask if any more important stories had surfaced about poor Herman's ghost.

The Evansville man waited for an answer. At last he got a letter from his Sauk Centre friend. When he opened the envelope it was empty. It seems that ghosts refuse to be betrayed. So, the mystery about Herman is safe for now.

The Man Who Named Honest Abe

Frederick Douglass was born 150 years ago to a Negro slave girl in Easton, Maryland. Few would have believed he would one day nickname a great president.

When Frederick was ten years old, he was sold at a slave auction to a shipbuilder in Baltimore. He worked in the shipyards for eleven years, then ran away. For the next few years, he did day labor wherever he could find it.

Words came easily to this young man and the Anti-Slavery Society soon took advantage of his quick mind and ready speech. It was at one of his lectures in New York that Mr. Douglass openly accused President Lincoln of being unnecessarily tardy in aiding the cause of the Negro.

A few weeks later, Frederick Douglass found himself standing on the steps of the White House in Washington, a single black speck among a sea of white faces. He wondered what their reasons for seeing the President might be. Had they, like him, been summoned too?

Frederick did not know what to expect, but he supposed that he would be the last one called to see the President that day. A hand on his shoulder jarred Frederick out of his thoughts and he looked up to see a White House messenger.

Hardly had he recovered before a second greater shock shook him. "The President will see you now, Mr. Douglass," the messenger said.

Frederick followed in a daze. To be ahead of all these white folks was surprising. For him, a black man, to be addressed as "Mr. Douglass" was unbelievable. He straightened his shoulders and held his chin high.

The door closed behind him and he was alone with President Lincoln who, as Frederick recalled later "gathered his feet from separate parts of the room," and stood to an amazing height. He offered Frederick a hand the size of a ham and a smile flickered across his tired face.

"Mr. Douglass, I know you; I've read about you. I took special note of what you said about me in a speech you made in New York."

"Yes, Mr. President. I'll explain anything I said the best I can." Frederick tried not to show how uneasy he really felt.

Sitting down again, the President laced his long fingers behind his head and leaned back. "You said that the most sad and disheartening thing about our present tragic situation, even worse than the disasters suggested by our armies, is the tardy and often changeable policy of the President of the United States."

Sensing that Mr. Lincoln had not finished speaking, Frederick remained quiet.

"Now, Mr. Douglass, I'll admit to being slow, and more often than not tardy, but not changeable. Once I've made up my mind I don't change it."

"In my opinion, Mr. President, you have been slow proclaiming equal protection for black soldiers and prisoners," Frederick said in a calm voice.

Slowly, Lincoln stood. Looking down at Frederick, he said, "To you, Mr. Douglass, I can see that my proclamation must seem slow in coming. A certain amount of talking has to be done first; but the proclamation will come!"

A ring of reporters waited for Frederick Douglass at the bottom of the White House stairs. Eagerly, they insisted that Frederick remember every gesture, every word. When he had finished telling about his visit, one of the reporters asked this final question: "What was your deepest impression of our President?"

Frederick Douglass

Frederick stood thoughtfully a full minute before he said, "I do not think Mr. Lincoln will go down in history as an Abraham the Great, or as Abraham the Wise, or Abraham the Eloquent. However, he is Abraham the Honest. Yes, he's an Honest Abe."

The reporters pounced on the nick name. To this day, Abraham Lincoln, our sixteenth president, is known affectionately all over the world as "Honest Abe."

Frederick Douglass named him.

*Humankind has not
woven the web of life.
We are but one thread within it.
Whatever we do to the web
we do to ourselves.
All things are bound together.
All things connect.*

Chief Seattle

Hunting Trip Gone Wrong

On Armistice Day, 1940, fourteen-year-old Ray Sherwin spent a long miserable night huddled together with two friends, Cal and Bob, under an overturned skiff. They were soaked. Without a fire their cotton pants froze to their legs. While this hunting trip cost Ray half of one foot and six weeks in the hospital, he survived only because he was the one in the middle with a friend on either side of him. Their warmth kept him alive. The next morning, 20 duck hunters were found frozen in anguished poses between Red Wing, Minnesota, and LaCrosse, Wisconsin.

On the morning of the hunt, when his mother told him storm warnings were up, Ray said, "The better to bring ducks down," and headed for Prairie Island spillway on the down end of Winona pool, where Ray's dad kept his boat. They decided to hunt three or four miles upstream, on the Upper Mississippi Wildlife Refuge, clamped on an ailing three-horse motor, and pulled out into choppy water.

The wind was sharp, with a sting, and dark clouds tumbled over each other overhead, but the boys were concentrated only on shooting ducks. They were dressed more for a picnic than a winter hunt Cal had a raincoat, but Bob and Ray had no protection. Beyond their boots, they had nothing more than a folder of matches. Had they paid attention, they could have read the weather by the irregular frenetic ways the duck were flying, turning, and twisting.

The river was two or three miles wide. It took the three boys almost two hours to wallow through the choppy water to their destination, a spot called "firing line." Deciding that it was too crowded at firing line, where blinds were less than twenty feet from each other, they moved on to a spot covered with willows next to a marsh.

When a booming wind began peppering them with sleet and powdery snow, they lost interest in hunting and moved to the willows, chilled to the bone. Two hunters who came by in a duck boat admitted they were scared. It was later revealed that the other boat had swamped. Its occupants were found standing frozen in waist deep water. The boys had no idea where they were and began to worry they would not be able to land the boat. In the icy wind, their gloveless hands were stiffening. In the open water, the boat nearly swamped. Then the outboard stopped and would not start again.

Cal tinkered with it, but his hands were so numb and stiff he cold not feel anything. The boys gave up on the dead motor and rowed. They could no longer see the boat ahead of them. They yelled but no one answered.

The storm washed their boat ashore. Ray was in the stern, still working with the motor, when a six foot wave smashed over the boat, soaking him to the bone. Ray tried to stand but his legs would not hold him, so he crawled across the mud, then just lay there, not caring. Cal and Bob dragged the boat to dry land, emptied out the water, and propped up one side for shelter. Ray crawled under it, the ice on his pants crackling.

They did not know where they were, only that they had never been here before. They did not talk much. Bob and Cal helped Ray all they could. They gathered rushes and spread them on the ground under the boat. Desperately, they looked for wood and finally they found two pieces of water-soaked drift wood. They drained gas from the tank to pour on it, but to no avail, since a vicious wind snatched the gas away before they could catch it. Soon the tank was dry and they had no fire. They covered themselves with their thin jackets, with Ray's raincoat on top. The last match flared. Bob and Cal crowded under the boat.

Then it got dark. Bob spoke a time or two during the night, concerned how his parents must be worrying. Ray prayed to himself for help. They were in deep trouble, but they were not dead. Life was still in them, if help would just come now. Ray realized that he could not feel his numb feet, which

felt like they were made of wood. The wind was like a wild thing, screaming crazily as it roared past them. Then Bob recalled that he had three apples in a pocket. They were frozen hard as baseballs, but gnawing them seemed to make them warm.

There was a sound. Was it a shot? No matter, their own guns were too crusted in ice even if they had been able to handle them. They realized that other hunters must also be in this fearful state. That help would soon be out looking, but not until the wind went down. Would that be too late?

Later, Ray found out that there were rescue boats out that same night. Men fought the storm in row boats all night long. Some even waded icy sloughs. For the hunters waiting for help, it was an unbelievable night. Some lived, others died. One lucky hunter got a fire going and burned 40 decoys. He lived to tell about it. Rescuers found hunters in the marsh near a fire they got going by shooting branches high up off trees. Two others, blinded by the storm, died only 400 yards from a fire, not knowing the fire was there. A few victims drowned. Twenty men died, but not all of the missing were accounted for.

When a murky dawn finally arrived, it was a different world. The wind had gone down, but the boys were in a horrible condition. Cal and Bob could hardly stand, and Ray had to be helped to his feet. It was as if they had no hands, but they worked to finally get in the boat. When they caught a glimpse of Winona's dam a few miles away, they knew where they were. After a struggle to get the boat over the high rim of ice that surrounded the lake, they rowed slowly out into open water, but lost control when they were unable to control the boat because their

hands were so stiff. Spray froze to the boat and as it grew heavier with ice it was swept across the Winona pool to the Wisconsin side.

They should have found safety here, but the marsh was frozen. Unable to make it across a new batch of ice, which tore a big hole in the boat but would not bear a man's weight, they sat huddled in the boat. An hour later, Max Conrad of Winona, flying a cub trainer plane, spotted them. He flew low over the boys, waggled his wings, and dropped cigarettes and sandwiches. He saw many empty boats, deserted gear and stranded dogs.

Before long they heard the roar of a power boat, the Chippewa. It could not reach them because the water was too shallow, so rescuers had to get a skiff. Later, Ray's dad and a friend showed up in a light boat with a powerful motor. They carried Ray to the launch and peeled off his clothes. His shoes were frozen to his feet. They gave him a slug of whiskey, even if he was only 14. Cal went home that same afternoon, but Bob spent a week in the hospital because of frozen hands. Ray had a tougher time. Gangrene set in and he lost a part of one foot. His weight plunged from 143 pounds to 85.

Ray, who became a teacher in LaCrosse, has hunted ducks more times that he can remember since that night in the Mississippi bottom slough, but now he takes the extra gear he sorely needed that awful night in 1940. Besides insulated boots, he takes a first aid kit, candy bars, matches, a knife, a set of extra warm clothing, and even a flare gun. He always tells people, "I will never again go hunting without that kit. There are too many mistakes to be made in this world without making the same one twice!"

Old Crow Wing - *The Once Vital Ghost Town*

Courtesy of Old Crow Wing State Park

Probably few other pieces of real estate have changed so much in a mere century and a half as has Minnesota, from a territory of trackless wilderness to statehood. There was a time not so long ago when Crow Wing, located on the road from Duluth to St. Paul to Fort Ripley where carts stopped to transfer cargo to wagons headed for the capitol, was the northern-most European settlement. A bustling little city, it was expected to become one of Minnesota's more important cities, the only one sitting at the confluence of two major waterways.

Clement Beaulieu, half Ojibwe and half French, came from Fond du lac (now Duluth) in 1848 to take over the Hudson Bay Company's Old Crow Wing agency. Dreaming of making Crow Wing the head of the American fur trade business, he foresaw streets alive with attractive tight little homes, with several denominations of churches, schools, a court house, a busy industrial section, and parks along the scenic rivers. To demonstrate his faith in the town, he built a home there.

When beaver hats lost ground in Europe the Crow Wing Trading Post began a long sure slide into history, although Crow Wing enjoyed a sporadic rejuvenation when there was a run on the buffalo robes that were much in demand by those who rode those cold Red River carts between St. Paul and Pembina. The real blow to Crow Wing occurred when the Northern Pacific Railroad laid track eight miles north of Red Wing at a place known today as Brainerd, despite the efforts of Clement Beaulieu, who from time to time locked horns to no avail with those who laid out plans for the Northern Pacific Railroad.

Beaulieu tried to keep his dream alive, but as trading stopped, the population faded away. Indian families moved to the White Earth Indian Reservation, leaving only the names of their dead on headstones in the Crow Wing Cemetery.

As the lights of Crow Wing dim while those in Brainerd grow brighter, let no one forget that Crow Wing and Clement Beaulieu were the ones who provided the spark.

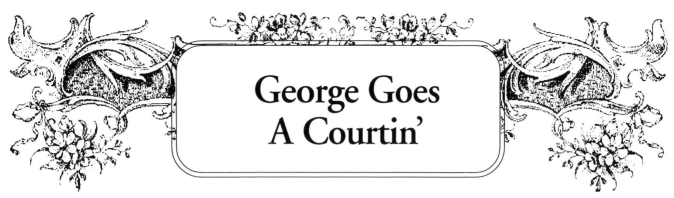

George Goes A Courtin'

Whistling "Standing On The Promises," George unhitched Dan and Nellie. Harness jingling, he drove them to the barn and slapped their dusty behinds into stalls.

George was a bachelor. There was talk of his sparkin' Hattie, Fred Leyh's girl, who possessed the loudest, highest voice in the Methodist Church.

George took a bath with brown soap, shaved, and applied corners of the Montgomery Ward Catalog to the places where he had knicked himself. In clean faded clothes, with his hair slicked down with glycerin water, and with his shoes blackened by an application of lard and stove-black, he was ready.

A final peek in the corner of a cracked mirror showed a missed sickle-shaped patch of week-old whiskers, but he was already late. It would have to do. Checking for matches, he grabbed the lantern. It would be dark when he came home.

George took the short-cut, which led back through both pastures and was a mile shorter than the road. Hattie, a little thing with soft brown eyes, opened the plank door.

George could never manage to slide his chair close enough to hers to hold hands until a half-hour short of ten o'clock, going home time according to Hattie's Pa. Kerosene wasn't cheap, he reminded them, and with five daughters a man had to be careful.

Finally, George pecked Hattie's cheek, gave her hand one last meaningful squeeze, and stepped out into the dark, thankful for the lantern. An inch of crystallized snow squeaked with every step.

George had cleared the last cowyard fence when he heard the first cry. Wolves! Over behind Peterson's Hill, but George knew there would be more. Before farming, he had spent years as a lumberjack. Two wolves answered from near Uncle Newt's barn. Before their cry had faded, three or four

George & Hattie

more replied, now from this side of Peterson's Hill. Then a much larger pack behind George's place started up. With each cry they tightened the circle, with George in the middle!

George started to run. He could hear what sounded like footsteps on the snow. Looking over his shoulder for red eyes, he forgot that the path swerved and hit a tree full force. The impact knocked him flat, blew out the lantern, and left him gasping for breath. Now it was pitch dark. Luckily, George's wire-rimed spectacles landed on his face, though they now fit his chin. He jammed them in his shirt pocket.

Sitting quietly, he listened. Didn't hear a

single thing. Likely crawling on their bellies. Wolves were smart, they were. You stop; they stop. He'd heard stories up in the woods. Jumping up, George rounded the tree and took off as if jet propelled. Yep, just like he thought--the varmints were back on his trail. He could easily hear them padding ever closer. George never realized the path was so crooked or so long.

The pack was ridiculously close now. Was that breath on his pants leg? If he was still alive in the morning, George resolved, he would get himself a dog.

At last, out of breath, George made out the peak of his barn, then the tall tree near the pump. The devils were waiting until the last moment to make their kill. Wolves did that. He wondered who would tell Hattie and how she would take it.

Then George rammed into his own back door with so much force it flew open, sending him sprawling into the middle of the kitchen floor. He kicked the door shut and yanked the wooden bolt into place. Shedding shoes that had rubbed his feet raw, he collapsed gasping for breath on his bed, hardly believing he had actually made it.

Relieved and exhausted, George was soon soundly asleep. It was full daylight when he opened his eyes. Slowly, he flexed one stiff limb after the other carefully. Gently, he swung his legs over the side of the bed, where his shoes lay, gaping widely as if laughing at him.

Scratching his head, George comforted himself with the fact that shoes couldn't talk. He would say he got all these bumps when he cut down a tree and keep his cap on as much of the time as he could. Hobbling to the door, George opened it.

Not a wolf track to be seen. When it became clear to George what had happened, all he could do was shake his head and wonder out loud if Hattie would still be interested in a fellow *who chased himself home?*

George did win Hattie as his wife and they had many years together. He was also instrumental in helping put this country together, serving many years on county and township boards. His influence is still felt in some areas. Their children were Edward and Leora.

Clay County Neck Tie Party!
The Swinging Of Thomas Brown

Not much was known about Thomas Brown, aged 26. Maybe his name wasn't "Brown," or he wasn't 26. It was known that a good part of his adult life had been spent in the Dakota Territorial Prison, where he was known as "Tommy Ryan." In Wisconsin, he had still another moniker.

In 1888, during the harvest season, a bunch of drunken hobos got into a brawl near Hillsboro, North Dakota. One was shot and killed. A local farmer gave Fargo police an accurate description of the killer, who was later identified as Brown. Fargo police spotted Brown and kept him under surveillance until he disappeared on October 17. Shortly after midnight, he reappeared at a dance in Moorhead, where an off-duty Fargo policeman name Benson pointed him out to Moorhead Patrolman Thompson. When Brown saw them talking, he pulled a gun and marched the officers down the stairs. At the foot of some steps, Benson jumped into the hotel bar behind an ice box. Thompson was told to walk down the sidewalk until they reached the Great Northern Railroad tracks. While this was happening, a citizen named Gleason, who had seen Brown draw a gun and march the officers downstairs, found Patrolman Pete Poull and told him Thompson was in trouble.

Poull hurried up 8th Street, coming on to Brown from the left, who saw Poull, cursed, and fired. Poull was hit in the heart. Crying, "My God! I am hit." Poull fell and died. Thompson then shot Brown once with his .38. Brown got off two shots at Thompson, then ran east to the railroad tracks, firing. He missed Thompson again, who responded twice, hitting Brown once. By now Brown's revolver was empty and he was severely wounded in the shoulder and leg. He surrendered and then collapsed between the rails. He was taken to the Clay County Jail, where the Law Enforcement Center is now.

There was rumor of a lynching so Sheriff Jorgan Jensen hustled Brown to the Hennepin County Jail in Minneapolis. Jensen guessed right; about midnight a large crowd of armed men with wrecking bars headed for the jail. Officers finally convinced them that Brown was gone by letting five men search the jail.

When tempers cooled, Brown was returned to Clay County Jail. A reporter for a local newspaper, *Argus*, submitted the following article:

"Surrounding cells are steel near a corridor about 5 feet wide. The cells themselves are 7 feet high. On top of these at the north end is the dungeon, or steel cage. The only light comes from diamond shaped holes between the heavy cross bars. The interior is about seven feet by nine feet, through the center extends a partition, dividing the room down the middle.

"In one of these little apartments, Brown has spent the lonely hours of his confinement, within easy sight of the little holes, has the gallows been erected, near the head of the stairs leading to the top of the cells. The gallows is in the southwest corner. It is created of pine. Two upright beams have a cross piece to which the rope will be attached. The rope is even with a platform and feet 3 inches above the top of the cells and about 2 feet square, so arranged that by moving a lever four slides are withdrawn and the drop falls, launching the condemned into space.

"From the top of the platform to the floor is nine feet, three inches for the drop of rope will be only seven feet. The rope is twelve feet long and a bit over a half-inch thickness. At the end is a hangman's knot, a peculiarly coiled one holding the loop. This will be kept in the Sheriff's safe until in use."

Local residents couldn't conceal their curiosity about the hanging. When an *Argus* reporter paid Brown a visit, he was amazed to see "several carriages in front of the jail." Inside both gentlemen and ladies standing around the gallows within only a few feet of Brown, who must have heard them, saying things such as, "I would hate to drop through that hole!" Another asked "I just wonder how Brown feels? Suppose the knot slipped and he strangled, ugh! Wouldn't that be awful?"

None of the comments bothered Brown, who bore up with the fortitude of a martyr. Perhaps to a hardened criminal time meant nothing. He visited with those assigned to spend the death watch with him and with those facing impending doom in the nearby cells. He only asked that all run smoothly. On his last day he slept away part of it and talked to the *Argus* reporter. He prayed with Father Augustine of St. Joseph's Catholic Church in Moorhead and Father Wolfgang from Luxembourg. He ate nothing. The Moorhead *Daily News* reported, "The law that was passed made it impossible for reporters to be there at an execution. Since the paper is a law abiding institution it will comply with the law."

The Fargo *Argus* complemented the Moorhead paper for its fortitude, then printed a detailed account. The Minneapolis *Tribune* printed that the *Argus* editor had one of the reporters arrested and thrown in jail in order to be sure of a front row seat at the hanging. He did not take into account that the unfortunate reporter was given a pail of water and a scrub brush. Instead of a front row seat for the hanging, he was on his knees scrubbing the ladies' room.

Curious citizens gathered at noon to be sure they were on time for the hanging at 4:30. The audience included the men from Fargo, the Coroner, an undertaker, the Cass County Sheriff Jensen and his assistants, Fathers Augustine and Wolfgang. Jailer Holgbeck and the two priests walked with Brown to the gallows. Brown kept his head up until the very end. He walked to the foot of the steps to the gallows then dropped to his knees. "I almost lifted him up on the platform," Holbrouk said. The Argus story said "Brown was standing between two priests, all in prayer, when the spectators came in. Brown's feet were tied, the noose was put on with the knot behind one ear. Brown shook hands with the Sheriff, jailer and priests and in a trembling voice wished them well. He nodded to the crowd, smiled, and the black cap was put on and fastened under his chin." A policeman and eight others tripped the trap.

Brown dropped at exactly 4:30 o'clock, and the one who shot Officer Poull swung into eternity. The fall broke Brown's neck, rendering him unconscious but not killing him immediately. Strangling followed, causing death. It took twelve and one-half minutes for his pulse to stop and his heart to stop beating.

This would be Clay County's only execution. It happened on September 10, 1889. Brown, or was it Ryan or somebody else, is out of the public eye at last, in an unmarked grave in the St. Joseph's Cemetery in Moorhead.

Thomas Brown

Patrolman Pete Poull (killed)

Clay County Jail

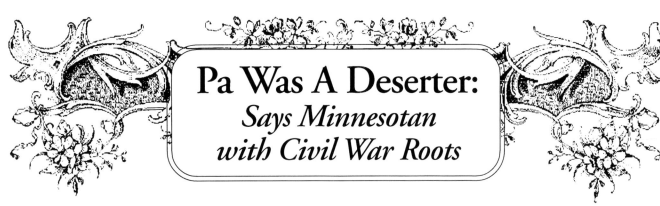

Mary Hitchcock shaded her eyes with her hand against a bright morning sun. She stood a minute longer looking east down a country road, then turned back toward the shack. This was the time of year Pa usually came dragging in. She hoped this year would be different. She hoped he wouldn't come. The boys worked hard this summer to have enough put up for the winter. Boys their age, 14 and 15, should be having fun. Going to ball games and such.

Mary had mixed feelings about Pa. His way of doing things was to stay over winter on their brush-country farm, then run like a pup with his tail in hot ashes when the roads opened up, more likely than not, leaving behind another baby on its way. Mary had eight now, not counting little Jason, who had died when he was four. A nice little kid Pa never even missed when he came back that fall three years ago. Didn't even ask until Sarah told him. That was the last straw. The boys had enough. Somehow, she couldn't blame them.

She had the best kids in the world. They shouldn't have to board a man and his horse, a man who had never turned a hand to help. On the other hand, she knew Pa, one of the most miserable of men, hadn't created his problem and would never rid himself of it as long as there was breath in his body.

Pa had lived in Illinois when he was a kid. He was fourteen and not a husky boy when the Union soldiers went through his family's yard. One of the soldiers leaned out of the saddle, grabbed Pa and rode off with him crying and yelling. Pa never saw his own folks again nor even dared to ask after them.

The army made a drummer boy out of pa. Pa was too scrawny to carry a heavy gun. Pa spent the next month, sick to his stomach, and in terror. Men standing next to him were torn in half by cannon balls. Some of them were beheaded. Horses screamed out a slow death in agony. The smell of blood never went away.

Then come the day he couldn't stand any more. During a march, they passed a field of scrub and Pa ran for it. The next months were a crazy haze for Pa. He laid low under brush piles in the woods during the day and ran shaking with fear at night, always hungry and cold. He knew the army never stopped looking for deserters and that the penalty for desertion was death by hanging. Pa kept running until he was in Minnesota, where he learned that the war was over. From what he could tell, people this far north didn't talk so much about it. The next three years were the most normal he would ever know.

Pa found a job as a hired man on a farm deep in tall timber. He fell in love with and married the farmer's daughter, Mary. It seemed like life was going to be all right. They had a little house of their own next to the big one. Mary planted a garden. Then one day a well-dressed salesman selling ointment stopped by. Pa freaked out. He was so sure the man was a scout looking for him, he hid in the barn and wouldn't come in until after dark. Next morning, Pa was gone. Mary waited for him to come back as long as she could, then went to stay with her folks to have her baby.

After a while she moved back to her little house. She put in a garden and did piece work for the neighbors, grateful she knew how to sew. Then one night after Pa had been missing two years, she heard something hit her bedroom window. It scared her half to death until she could realized it was Pa. Since staying out of sight on their place wasn't hard while the timber and brush were thick, Pa stayed until almost spring. When a man stopped by to water his horse, Pa took off again. Mary went to her folks to have the next baby.

This happened more than nine times. The two oldest boys took over milking the cows and

Mary Hitchcock

getting enough corn and hay up to feed their few stock over winter. They told a neighbor who helped a little that Pa was away in a hospital, awful sick. The girls helped in the garden and picked berries. Sometimes, Mary said to herself, "I'm raising a family of freaks. The kids are starting to act guilty, like they got caught sucking eggs. Like their pa. That's what living like this is doing to them." She puzzled night and day what she could do about it.

One day, as Mary was scrubbing clothes in the tub, her daughter Sarah came bounding through the door. Pushing long blond hair out of her face, she gasped, "Pa's coming! Got a different nag but I know it's him."

Mary went to look just as Pa turned in the drive. He looked so old she wondered if it was really him. His hair was almost gone and his overalls hung loosely on his frame. He looked as if he wouldn't weigh a hundred pounds. The boys, who looked up from where they were stacking hay in front of the

barn, never let on they saw him. Mary straightened her apron. In a voice she hoped didn't shake, she said "Hello, Fred. Mosquitoes sure bad for this late in the summer, ain't they?"

Pa glanced her way. "Tank got water in it?" he asked, leading his horse toward it. A grungy bundle done up in a shirt lay where he had tossed it. All his earthly belongings in it, Mary guessed. He stood on the far side of the horse so it was between him and the road, even if nobody hardly went on that road and you could hear them coming. The boys put down their pitch forks and came to stand beside Pa. Without looking up, he said "Howdy, boys."

"We ain't sayin' no howdy this year, pa." the oldest boy said. It's gonna be 'goodbye.' You've watered your nag, now move on. We ain't takin' winter boarders no more."

Like he'd never heard, Pa slapped the dust off his pants. "Not even goin' to let your Pa eat a bite?" he asked.

Shuffling his feet, the youngest boy said, "I guess nobody ever left here hungry. Ma sees to that. But after you've eaten you can leave."

Mary, in tears, turned back into the kitchen, wondering how a body could be on both sides of a fence the same time. She sliced deep into a tender ham she had been saving for Thanksgiving, beat up a half-dozen fresh eggs, and opened a jar of wild strawberry jam the girls had made. While Pa ate hungrily, she busied herself putting everything to eat she could put her hands on in a tied-up dish towel.

"I guess you want it this way, Mary?" Pa asked around a mouthful. Mary sat down opposite Pa with a cup of coffee.

"I don't blame the boys none or you either, Mary. It ain't been no kind of a life; I couldn't even give my kids a right name," he said.

"Not for you neither." Mary bit back tears. "You never asked for this. They just grabbed you."

"No, Mary girl, I know I sure didn't. Maybe I been too scared and perticklar--but I seen a feller hung one time. I'll be all right. I kind of know somebody else on the lam, maybe I kin go bunk with him." Pa took one more swallow of coffee, picked

up the dishtowel sack, and looked a long minute at Mary. Then he walked slowly toward his rig and without a backward look nor a wave of his hand drove off back down the dusty road he came on. It would soon be dark.

Life changed for the Hitchcocks. Anybody who asked about Pa was told he died. They started visiting neighbors and the boys took Ma to church. After a few years people stopped asking about Pa. They never really knew him anyhow; he was so queer somehow. Pa was never heard of again.

"I, Ethelyn Pearson, can tell this story the way it was told to me because 'Pa' was my great grandfather. The little girl Sarah was my grandmother. I recall an old lady sitting in a rocker in the corner of my grandma's kitchen. She wore a lace cap and was smoking a pipe. Her name was 'Mary Hitchcock,' or at least that is the name she went by."

23. The Hamburg Massacre in South Carolina, July 8, 1876, started a chain of events which profoundly affected political movements both locally and nationally.

Cannibalism Lurked Behind the *Real* Moby Dick

Both George Pollard and First Mate Owen Chase were flying high that August 12, 1816, morning. They had both been promoted and life was good. With a crew of 21, they sailed from Nantucket, Massachusetts in the cold Atlantic to a whaling grounds in the South Pacific for a stay as long as two and one-half years. They sailed in the Essex, an elderly craft that had come out of a session in dry dock that restored her like new. Essex was 87 feet long and weighed 238 tons, unladen. She had the aura of a lucky ship.

The Essex had been out only three days when a violent storm laid her far over on her side. The crew considered this an evil omen and wanted to go back, but Owen talked them into staying. No damage was done. Essex reached Cape of Good Hope on January 18, 1820. The water had been fearsome, threatening, every mile of the way. The sailors were uneasy again, but once they were in the Pacific they relaxed until November 16, when a boat was struck by a sperm whale's tail fluke. The boat was wrecked, leaving the Essex with only three good whaleboats. This type of accident was common.

Four days later, on November 20, there was more trouble. A giant whale, at least 85 feet long, swam along side, then suddenly turned and headed straight for the boat, ramming it so hard men on board were knocked down. It backed off, leaving a hole above the water line, then returned, hitting it this time below the water line. Satisfied, the whale swam away, but the boat was doomed. Returning, the crew was surprised to find the big ship sinking. The Essex rolled far over and lay on her side. It righted when they cut the masts. Swiftly, they plundered the ship for provisions and divided them between the three boats. The men estimated that it would take them 56 days to reach safety. They dreaded

the thought of landing on a South Pacific island for fear of cannibals.

The three boats pulled away from the sinking Essex on November 22 at 4:00 o'clock. The ship had sunk from sight. One of the boats, already needing repairs, was a liability. It was shipping water at an alarming rate. They tried to repair what they could. On December 20, they had gone 480 miles. There was no problem with provisions, and they sighted several small islands, but they were too small to keep 20 men. Three men decided to stay on an island and take their chances rather than starve at sea.

On December 17, the crew set sail again. Rations had been cut in half and the men were starved and in dire need of water. A man named Matthew Joy was the first to die. His body was committed to the sea. The next day a vicious squall separated the boats. On January 1, Richard Peterson died. On February 8, Isaac Cole died in terrible agony.

It was decided that the body be kept for food. The men sickened at the prospect, but agreed. Their grisly diet lasted until February 15. Spirits were down and they saw no hope. A British ship, the Indian,

picked up the three men on the island. The remaining two boats stayed together until January 14. Charles Shorter died and the next day Isaiah Shepherd died, followed by Samuel Reed. All of them provided food for the starving survivors.

The third boat containing three men were never seen or heard of again. On February 1, Pollard's load were starving. They all decided that lots would be drawn, with the unlucky one to be shot to feed the rest. It was Pollard's young nephew who drew the shortest straw. He was shot by Charles Ramsdell. On February 11, the whaling ship Dolphin pulled Pollard and Ramsdell from the sinking boat. They had been at sea 95 days in an open boat, traveling 3,500 miles.

George Pollard sailed one more time as captain of a whaling ship. In March of 1823, the ship piled up on a coral reef. He retired a broken man, serving out 45 years as a night watchman.

Benjamin Lawrence went on to captain two successful whaling ships, farmed a few years, and died at 80. Ramsdell captained the General Jackson before retiring from the sea, and William Wright was drowned in a hurricane in the West Indies. Seth Weeks is the only one who retired from the sea without making one more voyage. Chase made two more successful trips before retiring in 1840, due to ill health. He had to endure splitting headaches that doctors thought were due to the 1821 affair. He became mentally ill and died in March 1869, when he was 71. Chase wrote a short phamplet of his experience. A son told a man he met in a restaurant about it and gave him his father's manuscript.

That young man was none other than Herman Melville, who turned the piece into *Moby Dick*.

Sketch of the Essex being attacked, by Nickerson.
Courtesy, www.pbs.org

Moltan Hell Created the Creeping Molasses Disaster

On January 15, 1919, one hundred and seventy residents of a Boston suburb were pitched into an 8 or 15 foot deep flow of steaming, writhing molasses. Twenty-one of them died by drowning, being cooked, or both. This monster also swept a dozen horses along with it as well as everything else. Anything in its path became a victim, swallowed up and overcome at a speed of 35 miles per hour. It was not unlike descriptions of Armageddon.

Foreman Ray Smereage and his crew were loading the fifth train car on the track, but none of them survived. Three men eating their lunch in the shade of the monster tank were the first to go. Not only the people, but the houses they lived in, the cars they drove, all went. When Captain Krake of Engine 7 saw what seemed to be a victim he grabbed for it, pulling out the lifeless body of a little girl. There was a deep, unworldly kind of a roar that defied description. Life was never the same for those who somehow survived.

The culprit was a giant tank of hot molasses 90 feet across and 58 feet high. It was the property of the United States Industrial Alcohol Company to be used in the making of rum. It sat in the Charleston Navy Yard high above the freight sheds. Inside the tank 2,500,000 gallons of hot molasses rolled. It exerted 2 tons of pressure per square foot of cast iron tank. When the thermometer raised from zero to above forty degrees a steaming hissing flow of molasses exploded with enough force to blow a train from the tracks.

Men began pulling burned sticky bodies from the river of molasses that flowed by within minutes, when the alarm sounded at 12:40 noon. Nothing had prepared them for what awaited them. They worked as best they could in the searing brown serpentine mass. When it finally hit the ocean it writhed up into a sickening yellow foam.

Conversation flourished with theories as to why a vessel with plates like a battleship could fold like a toy. The explanation that seemed to make the most sense was that the mixture had begun to work and heat on its own. When the outside temperature climbed from zero to almost fifty degrees, fermentation took over and the mixture started to expand. Because of prohibition the tanks may have been overfilled.

Judge Hitchcock of Massachusetts courts appointed Cal. Hugh W. Ogden as auditor. At least 125 lawsuits against the United States Industrial Alcohol Company materialized. It was six years later that he made a  report. On that day the court was so crowded that only two claimants could be represented. The number of experts in engineering, metallurgy, along with a host of other sciences had never seen anything like it. For instance, Albert L. Colby, who was an expert in steel structural strain was on the stand for three weeks during ten hour days.

Upwards of 3,000 witnesses took the stand to fill 45,000 pages of copy. One group of witnesses denied the theory of structural infirmity and instead tried to prove there had been a dynamite bomb and sabotage by the company. It took more than six months for clean-up crews to wipe up the clinging mess. The smell of molasses still clung in a sickening wave to cobblestones.

The end of negotiations came with the plaintiffs winning the case.

Sabotage was not involved. The company had to make awards totaling more than a million dollars because the tank was filled to more than capacity and was insufficiently strong, or structurally weak. Did the rise in temperature play a part? That will always be debated in Boston.

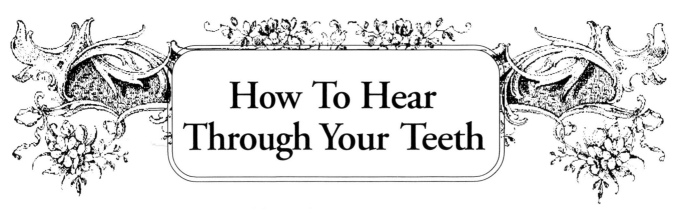

How To Hear Through Your Teeth

In 1894, R. S. Rhodes determined that nearly fifty percent of all children were hard of hearing, if not totally deaf. He believed that these children could be educated through the use of a mechanical aid which allowed them to hear through their teeth. Rhodes believed his "audiphone" could improve hearing thirty percent and bring many deaf children within reach of human voice and valuable speech. Hand one to deaf students, he contended, and they could hear and be educated.

Rhodes visited institutions in the United States and in Europe, carrying his device with him, claiming no other instrument would reveal harmonies like his. It was not only the best, he asserted, it was the only one. Any institution that did not provide an audiphone for their hearing-impaired students, he contended, was robbing them, sending ignorant children into the world from these institutions. It was a grievous offense which would never be forgotten or forgiven, and might deprive them of sheer joy and the ability to make a living. The responsibility, Rhodes argued, rested with educators. Would they be prepared to say, "We will stick to the old ways?" Or would they rise to the occasion and reap the blessings of future generations?

"As for me," Rhodes said, "I would rather be the innovator of this little device that serves commercial purpose."

Rhodes Audiphone

THE AUDIPHONE IS A NEW INSTRUMENT MADE OF A PECULIAR COMPOSITION, PROCESSING THE PROPERTY OF GATHERING THE FAINTEST SOUNDS (SOMEWHAT SIMILAR TO A TELEPHONE DIAPHRAGM) AND CONVEYING THEM TO AUDITORY NERVES THROUGH MEDIUM OF THE TEETH. THE EXTERNAL EAR HAS NOTHING WHATEVER TO DO IN HEARING WITH THIS WONDERFUL INSTRUMENT. Thousands are in use by those who would not do without them for any consideration. It has enabled doctors and lawyers to resume practice, teachers to keep teaching, mothers to hear voices of their children, thousands to hear a minister and attend concerts and theatre and engage in general conversation . Music is heard perfectly with it where without it not a note could be distinguished. It is convenient to carry and to use. Ordinary conversation can be heard with ease. In most cases deafness is not detected. Full instructions will be sent with each instrument. The audiphone is patented throughout the civilized world.

Miss Eastman and 'Many Lightenings'

Nancy Eastman was the daughter of Lieutenant Seth Eastman and a Dakota woman. When Seth was transferred, he left the Dakota woman behind, and later married a white woman named Mary. Eventually, he was transferred back to Ft. Snelling.

Nancy was raised traditionally by her Dakota grandmother. When she was seventeen, she fell in love with a handsome Indian brave and planned to elope. As she made her way to the appointed place, she was relieved to see that her beloved waited so they could get away before the dogs sounded an alarm. When she came up along side of him, he scooped her up with one strong arm to ride behind him. They moved off slowly so as not to draw attention. Well after midnight, they found an abandoned cabin, and stopped for the night.

Next morning, as the light of a new day crept through the holes in the wall of the shack, Nancy received a shock. She had spent the night, not with her lover, but with his best friend, a man named "Many Lightenings." Somehow he had gotten his hands on the message she had sent her lover, told him the meeting was off, and instead came himself. He had long admired Nancy and wanted her for himself.

Nancy considered it too late to return to her real love and so became the devoted wife of Many Lightenings. They had five children. Soon after the last one was born, Nancy became desperately ill. As she lay dying, she asked Many Lightening's mother to raise her son.

In 1862, Many Lightenings joined his tribe in a battle against the whites. He was captured and sent to prison. While there, he accepted Christianity and changed his name to Jacob Eastman. After Eastman was released, he started looking for his children. One by one he found some of them. His mother and youngest son were in Canada. Many Lightening renamed the boy Charles Alexander Eastman. Eastman, who studied medicine, later became famous for his books on growing up Dakota.

Stranded Pox Victims Become A Doctor's Dilemma

It was the hot summer of 1868 that a steamboat loaded with sick frightened people pulled up to the Red Wing wharf. One look at the stricken load on that boat and it was waved back into the middle of the river. Red Wing people could not be blamed for being terrified of contracting cholera, small pox or diphtheria. There was little or no help for any of the travelers. Whole families died, leaving no one to bury the rest. The only certain thing was that if you got any one of the plagues, you died!

Dr. Charles Hewett was the newest doctor in Red Wing. He had delt with all three diseases before. His first act was to order the boat back into the river and to unload on an island in the middle of the river. Where there was an empty house that he did his best to turn into a makeshift hospital. The Red Wing town council was generous in providing everything the stricken people needed. By doing so, not a single case made its way into Red Wing.

Dr. Hewett was instrumental in getting other doctors to join him to create a state board of health. He spent the next 20 years trying to make Minnesota a healthier place to live and rear a family.

In 1862, most people would rather stay home when they were ill than go to a hospital. Dr. William Mayo agreed. Then in 1883, a tornado hit the Rochester, Minnesota area leaving many dead and wounded people. When the nuns tried to care for them in a school they realized how badly a hospital was needed. The nuns went to Dr. Mayo with an idea, the Sisters of St. Francis would build a hospital if Dr. Mayo would be the doctor. He accepted the position and the hospital was called "St. Mary's." It eventually became the famous Mayo Clinic and included a school for nurses.

Dr. Hewett did not live to see the time when sick people with a disease like diptheria were quarantined at home, instead of letting it spread. Minnesotans had learned that vaccinating was the answer.

Dr. Charles M. Hewett

An 'X' Took Our Home

A piece written by Caroline Blais Rose describing her childhood and grandchildren.

I am Caroline Blais Rose. I was born at home in a farm house dad built. This was south of Swanville, Minnesota, in Todd County, on April 18, 1918. There were 11 of us between the ages of newborn and twenty-three. My dad, who we called "Pa" was thin, spoke very broken English and was very neat. He spoke flawless French. All the trees on the place were planted by him. It was a beautiful wind break. When a man from Iowa told him his grove was depleting the soil of things plants needed, upon hearing this, he set to chopping the grove down the next day. He planted cedar, plum, pin cherries, high bush cranberries, and raspberries. Also, rhubarb.

Dad built a big two story house. We were all born in it. It was a nice house with big rooms. Each of the three bedrooms could hold three double beds. We were near a lake and could see those wonderful Minnesota sunsets from our kitchen window. No plumbing, but sort of a sewer system. Our sink had an under ground pipe that just washed the water down hill. Our kitchen stove was a big Monarch. Its oven door was split in the middle horizontally. Part of it went half up and the other half down. It had a big copper reservoir so there was always hot water. It was a steady job in a family of 13 to keep it full. It had an oven that held 12 loaves of bread at one time. Mom always baked beans the same time. Dad's chair faced the kitchen door so he cold see everybody, coming or going.

This chair could twist either up or down. We didn't dare set in it. Dad also had his own knife and fork. The knife was very sharp. Both had a bone handle, "The fork had three tines. Spoons were kept in a spoon holder in the middle of the table. It was the fanciest dish on the table. No electricity in our house, but we had some pretty lamps. I especially liked a pull-down Aladdin. It had two mantels. We also had a squat lamp on the wall with a movable reflector behind it. It was handy for school work as it could make one spot very bright. They all burned kerosene and had to be filled every day and the chimneys washed. That was my job and I hated it. They broke so easy.

Our beds were something else. The beds themselves were beautiful.....spring and mattresses quite something else. They were all double beds and went down in the middle like hammocks. There were 3 in a bed. You better hope you were in the middle. Corn husks that had been dried filled the mattresses and ticks. They were sewed in. I know only of uncomfortable beds. Mom made our quilts of different shaped pieces on a flour sack. She would embroider around each piece. The wool in the middle had to be carded. We had one dresser that was so pretty. It had little shelves halfway up on each side of the mirror with carved out grapes underneath. When we played church we used it for our alter.

Our big "King 8" car was housed in the machine shed. It was a long car. It had a front seat and a back seat with lots of room between. There were two seats folded up on the back of the front seats that folded down. When they were not used a sort of curtain came down to hide them. Our buggy was stored there, too. It was a beauty. When the folks went to the neighbors to play cards we took this buggy down to the cow pasture and rode it down the hills.

Our first barn was an eyesore. I don't think it ever saw a drop of paint. It had a long slanted tin roof. We used it for our slippery slide when it was wet. The new barn was tall with a mansard roof. It had shingles and an upstairs cement floor. Dad didn't want any dances to be held there. The hay mow had a rail running in the peak called a "hay track". It is used to bring bundles of hay off racks and into the mow. It was good to do acrobatic stuff on. Then dad caught us and we quit. He said it was lucky we didn't break our necks.

Our horses were beautiful animals with stalls in one end of the barn. Chub was a reddish color and Charlie was black. Also, we had Dick, a black

horse with a white face. He was slow....or was he smart? We never figured it out. One day our nephew, age four, went to the barnyard to play. Dick just walked over, picked him up by the collar and lifted him back over the fence to safety.

Springtime was maple time. We were a busy family. We made maple syrup and sugar to sell. That's when those special buckets would come down from the attic along with sugar molds and the big copper boiler. Everything had to be washed. The trees were four miles from home in my oldest brother's woods. To tap a tree you had to bore a hole in it and drive in a kind of spigot that had a notch on the end to hold the bucket. The sap, as clear and thin as water, went drip, drip drip into the bucket. It tasted like sweetened water. On the larger trees we sometimes put two taps.

Dad and older boys would tap from 400 to 1,000 trees. We would have barrels in our wagon and dump sap in them. This maple business was done in the cold Minnesota spring and gathering the sap and riding back and forth in the horse drawn wagons was cold. There was no place to warm up and our feet were both wet and cold. When we had a load we would take it back to the farm and strain the sap into a large metal tank. Not too far from the house was this boiling pan. It was about 12 feet long and 5 feet wide. Pa would have the sap run in that slowly. It was partitioned off so that he could have a thinner sap that needed more and faster boiling on one end, and sap that was beginning to thicken and become sugar on the other so it could be removed, strained into clean cans and brought into the house to "finish off". Some was cooked a little longer to be made into sugar.

My mother tested it by bringing in a pan of snow and pouring tablespoonfuls of maple sugar into it. Was THAT good! You can bet we had a lot of company at that time of year. Some came to buy, some for the free taffy pull, some for the free samples from the broken sugar molds. We stored maple sugar in a chest to sell and also for our summer use. The sugar was made into rounds from divided molds and some from muffin tins. This was the time for

pancakes, too. We scrapped loose sugar off a loaf, sprinkled it on a pancake with butter, and rolled them up and ate them. I think we invented "crepes".

It seems like so many tasks were mother's. She was the only one who did the milking and separated the milk. This was done by a machine that you turned by the handle. The milk was strained and poured into a large metal bowl that sat on top and then it ran through the separator bowl, which was about 20 discs encased in a metal case. As the milk went through, the cream would come down one spout and skim milk in another one. Now, this thing had to be washed and boiled every day. It was an AWFUL job.

Mother did all the canning. Jars and lids had to be washed and boiled. All fruits were done the open kettle method and vegetables, cold packed. It made the big old stove roar and the kitchen got hotter and hotter. Pretty soon mother turned white and started having chills that made her teeth rattle. We put her to bed with lots of blankets on that hot day with a cold towel on her head. She didn't feel well for a week.

To get butter we had this big keg on a stand. My mother would put the cream in and start to turn it. You watch for grains of butter to appear on a glass spot on the lid. You churn, then you churn some more until it starts going clump, clump, from side to side. That's when it is time to drain the buttermilk off. This is done from a hole on the side as big as a nickel. Once when I was in charge of holding the churn still while that milk drained off, I decided to start churning. Needless to say, we had buttermilk all over the kitchen.

I have told you about our breakfasts, with the pancakes. Seldom did we have oatmeal. There was a time, I guess, that was the beginning of the depression. Dad's cousin who worked at Pillsbury mills brought us oatmeal, and flour. For the noon meal we always had homemade vegetables with all of those vegetables we canned, beans, peas, and tomatoes. We ate this with bread. We ate everything with bread. Mother made the best in the country.

Our evening meal was usually fried potatoes. We boiled them with jackets on earlier then fried or boiled pork and vegetables. Desserts were canned fruit sauce always eaten with bread. Sometimes we had bread pudding. Mom would make a vanilla or lemon sauce topping. We went to bed early. It saved fuel, kerosene for lamps, and to heat the house.

The only time I can remember having cake is when my oldest sister, Esther, came with her 4 kids from Illinois. She would make chocolate cake from sour cream with whipped cream on it. What a treat! When supper was over and dishes done, mom would read the paper, sometimes out loud so Dad could hear as he couldn't read. He had never gone to school. One time she was reading to herself and I was in back of her so I could see to read. There in big black letters , it said "The End Of The World!". I went to bed and cried my eyes out.

Then it was 1933 with the depression in full swing. Everyone was poor. When I was in my second year of high school my folks lost the farm. What a sad day! It was a shady deal from the bank. On some of the bank notes there was just an "x" indicating that was how pa could sign a check. Actually, mother had taught pa to write his name so he could do it properly when necessary. He never signed an x. It was too late and everything was gone by the time this was discovered. This con game the bank played didn't help them much because they soon had to close the doors, too. We could have squeaked by.

All they had worked for so hard those long years was gone. The folks rented a scrubby run-down house in town. It was so little we couldn't all be home the same time. Farming was all they knew how to do. It was too late to start over.

Courtesy of Long Prairie Historical Society

Preachers Do Too!

I will never forget that soft, summer night when it was my lot to have to attend a bible school program with the young preacher. I do not recall why my parents could not go, but I DO remember that ride! After the program, the preacher took the other kids that rode along home, but he forgot that I was left in the car. I had fallen sound asleep in his back seat....

Softly spoken mumbled words worked their way into my world of deep sleep until I opened my eyes. Where was I? I was in the back seat of a car but...whose was it? Where were we? Hushed talk came freely from the front seat. It was obvious "they" did not know I was here. I lifted my head off the bristly cushion and looked. It was dark. A red fall moon filtered enough light so I could see figures. No details, but they sure liked each other, I could tell that. Now I could see big tree trunks so close it looked like they were leaning on the car. Where in the Land of Goshen was I? How in tarnation did I get here? I was seven and I sure didn't know what to do!

It was definitely a man and a woman. I heard a small slapping sound and the man said "Aw, are the naughty old skeeters bitin' my baby?" I wondered what he was talking about. She was definitely no baby! There was enough light for me to see THAT. Another louder slap and the same voice said in a triumphant tone, "There! Got"im. Don't want any mean old skeeter chewin' on my doll." She kind of breathed a whispery word I couldn't hear. Then he said "I know, the air is close with the windows all up. I'll turn one down a bit." She said that whispery word again.

It got quiet. How was I going to get back to grandma's? We lived in Minneapolis but my dad was here helping grandpa with something. Grandma was a nut about my going to what she called "Bible School" while I was here. I didn't know a soul. I was glad when it was program night even if I had to ride with two other kids and the preacher. Whoever the man called his "baby" in the front seat laid her head on his shoulder. He said "Honey Bun, you're shivering. Here, let's get this jacket around you. If I get out from behind this stearing wheel you can climb right up here on my lap." I eased my head back down on the seat. I couldn't place her, but THAT was the preacher's voice sure as shootin' !

I could see out the back window that the moon was straight up. Grandpa and Grandma lived halfway between Sebeka and Menahga. I was tall for my age and it was cramped. Chilly, too. If we stayed much longer the preacher was going to have a puddle in the back seat. The preacher let out a little yelp. "Why, you little rascal. I do believe you bit my ear!"

They laughed like nobody ever bit anybody's ear before.

The preacher started to sing in his thin voice "He leadeth me in..............." when all of a sudden my dilemma was settled. Dew on grass and bushes and stuff always made me sneeze and he had rolled the window down. I sneezed before I could pinch my nose, I nearly blowed my ear drums out.

Well, you should have been there. The preacher jumped 'til he dumped her on the floor. She hit the top and the rear view mirror came clatterin' down. I moaned a little like I do when I am just waking up. I peaked a bit and came close to laughing. Both of them were hanging their chins over the top of the front seat trying to figure out who I was. "That's the Johnson girl," he whispered. She said, "Huh uh, more like the Linnell girl. She's taller." NOW I knew who baby was. A hot-shot teacher from St. Cloud came yesterday to help our country teachers put on the program. She had a howly voice and the way she banged it you would never have guessed our old piano was out of tune. She taught us to say "I weel make you feeshers or men, feeshers of men......" I admired the way she wore a neck scarf in her hair. It didn't look so good now, all crooked.

They decided on something because the car started and without lights we crept out of somebody's woods. She was way over by the door now. Talking louder so I could hear they said how it sure was a long program. After a ways on gravel and a paved road they pulled into grandpa's drive. Grandma had all three kerosene lamps lit and the lantern on the back stoop. Taking my hand the preacher led me down the path to the back door. It flew open and four worried faces looked out. The preacher handed me in, saying how the car was taking too much gas these days and how it run out. He said they should be proud of me I was a wonderful little girl and would make a fine woman some day. Then he backed out and high tailed it back to the car.

Everybody crowded around me. Where had we run out of gas? Did the poor preacher have to walk far? Did they give him the gas for free or did he have to pay? I said "I don't know, I don't know, I don't know. I didn't see them put in gas out in the woods."

"Woods!" my mother said.

"Yeah. What woods?" Dad asked.

"The woods they were neckin' in." I was getting tired.

Now grandma got into it. "They who? And what do you mean, 'neckin'?"

"I don't know w…hat woods. But it was neckin' when they were snugglin' an' she bit his ear and stuff. She's the one who helped with the program." I started for bed.

Grandma said "Girl, girl, how can you talk thataway about a reverend? Why, he never parked in the dark in the woods in his life!" Dad and grandpa each let out a hoot that woke my little sister. Mom called "You say your prayers tonight, young lady. Twice!" The next morning grandma read to me what the bible had to say about liars.

A couple of days went by and we were getting ready to go home. I went out to get the mail for grandpa one last time. There, on the bottom of the front page was that preacher and his doll's picture! They were getting married. I ran to grandma with it and shoved it right up close under her nose so she didn't even need to change glasses. She said "Hmmnn, make a nice couple don't they?"

I stomped out to the car.

Jane Eli

In 1863, during the Civil War, Jane and Edward Eli of Wabaska, Minnesota were among the few parents affluent enough to afford a visit to their stricken son in the hospital at Broad and Cherry Streets in Philadelphia. Jane took it upon herself to call on all of the boys from Minnesota, if possible. It was said 14 soldiers from Minnesota died the preceeding weekend. Jane was successful in finding her son, Charles Eli, and Charles Goddard. Jane Eli was instrumental in getting Minnesota boys transferred to hospitals in Minnesota.

A letter to her mother on July 2, 1863, reads:

My Dear Mother,

I have arrived here on Wednesday morning safe and sound and have succeeded so far in all that we planned. I was immediately sent to General Head Quarters and made proper inquiries. After some questions I found our boy. I can't tell you how surprised and happy he was. He is healing as fast as possible. Charlie was wounded very badly. The physician considered it hopeless and left him to die. Doc's don't waste time or medicine on soldiers with less than "half a chance to live in their favor. They make that decision in one quick glance as they walk by, and our Charlie was one of those walked by. He bled nearly to death and one of the Minn. boys told me about him being passed by. It's a great wonder he lived. A drummer boy noticed him and seven others and got them in a hospital. He was so saturated with blood he was obliged to take his pants off and went without. He had to wrap a blanket around him. I can't say too much for the drummer boy. They were in a Baltimore hospital.

When they came to this hospital in Philadelphia Charlie was very weak and was considered the worst case among them. He is much better and got a pass yesterday and walked out for the weekend. I am going to get him back to Minnesota one way or another. The Physician told me that all the boys here want to be transferred to a Minn. State Hospital. Charles says to tell you hello.

Your daughter Jane

(extract from private letter}
July 2, 1863
Dear Husband,

I have at last arrived at the hospital and found our boy without too much difficulty. He is surprised and delighted to see me. A Mr. Marvin in the next bed got hold of my hand and I thought he would never quit shaking it. Our Charlie is weak, but is able to get up a bit. The field doctors thought he was mortally wounded and would do nothing for him until a drummer boy whose name he doesn't know took off his blood soaked clothes and put a blanket around him and into a hospital. He was in a Baltimore hospital over night where some nice ladies provided him and others with clean dry clothes and dressed their wounds. He says to tell you hello and misses you, as do I.

Your loving wife, Jane

July 12, 1863
Dear Mother,

I cannot write anything very encouraging about Charles he has been getting worse every day since I wrote last. When I first came he seemed to be doing well, his wound was healing fast and we all thought in a little while he would be nearly as well as ever. He was not allowed to be away since he was taken with fever sickness at the stomach and loss of appetite. I asked a doctor if sickness was caused by

his wound or by a cold. Charles thought it was a cold. The doctor thought the same. While we thought he was doing so well, matter was accumulating inside and instead of a poultice to draw it out, the wound was allowed to heal shut. If he had been left in the hospital without someone to take a real interest in him, he would be beyond caring by now. I am glad I came!!

Poor Charlie Goddard is wasting away. I checked with a Dr. about him who said he had a very bad wound. I think he was neglected too long. I wish that his mother could have come 2 weeks ago. Cases are too often left with just nurses. The physicians will collect around his bed and pour medicine when they know it is too late. Two more died on this ward last night. I am tired so will close. Rest assured I am watching over our Charlie.

Your daughter, Jane

July 30, 1863
Dear Husband,

I am a bit better rested but will go to the hospital in a bit. I have kept at them and was told that Minnesota hospitals are getting ready for them, so all Minn. boys from here will soon be home. They will be going to a State Hosp. They refused to give Charlie Goddard a transfer as they say his wound is too near an artery…that a jog in a train might be the end. He wants to come so bad to get another Dr.'s opinion. I do not want to be the one who tells him.

At least I found out yesterday that the graves of the fallen at Gettysburg were all marked. Take heart…as we will soon be home.

Your loving wife, Jane

BROAD STREET U.S. GENERAL HOSPITAL
On the site of present Parkway Building, Broad and Cherry Streets

Skinned Alive

John Mankins was an ornery cuss, no doubt about it. But perhaps even someone like Mankins rated better than being skinned alive by a pack of Indians. On the other hand, Mankins had asked for it.

In 1853, Mankins, who had been living in the Flippin Barrens between Yellville, Arkansas, and the White River, left Marion County, Arkansas, to join two parties of emigrants traveling together as insurance against an Indian attack. This Mankins had a reputation of being overbearing and disagreeable, and had once come within the width of a felt hat of killing a hunting companion.

Bill "Fatty" Jones and William C. Roberts had organized a bear hunt and invited Mankins along. When they chased a bear into a cave, Mankins, with a rifle, was stationed at the mouth to keep back the dogs and shoot the bear when he came out. Jones and Roberts went into the cave, with Fatty carrying a rifle and William carrying a torch.

Inside, the cave narrowed. The bear saw the light, made a wild run for the entrance, and knocked the torch out of Bill's hand. Fatty, black bushy hair waving, gave up the hunt and headed for the entrance on all fours, where Mankins, fortunately not on target, blew a hole in Jones' hat. Without waiting to enjoy the cussing Jones gave Mankin, the bear faded into the woods. It was the last time Mankins was invited to hunt bear with them.

As the trains approached the frontier, Mankins began to boast that he would shoot the first Indian he saw. Recognizing the danger he posed to the train, the other emigrants tried to reason with Mankins, but he paid no attention, finally carrying out his boast as they passed an Indian encampment comprised solely of women and children. Mindlessly, Mankins raised his gun and killed an Indian woman.

The emigrants moved on, with the rising expectancy that when the Indian men returned to the encampment and discovered the crime, the train would be in danger. Sure enough, on the fourth day

following the murder, they saw an approaching cloud of dust, which turned out to be at least 100 warriors in full war paint and feathers. With no patience to parley, the warriors surrounded the train and demanded the murderer. The emigrants were not reluctant to comply. Trembling with fright and blabbering nonsense, Mankins was handed over to the avengers.

Mankins was quickly stripped naked and tied to a wagon wheel with sixty feet of rawhide rope. After sharpening their knives, the Indians went to work. Starting at his neck, they began skinning Mankins alive. The rope was unwrapped as they made their way down his body, taking his skin, not in patches or stripes, but in one piece, like a man takes off his long johns. Mankins' screams of pain and terror wavered over the fields, curdling the blood of the emigrants, who had been forced to witness the skinning.

Mankins begged, cussed, prayed, all to no avail. When the Indians were done, they cut loose his bloody, quivering body, letting it fall where it landed. They then rolled up the skin, tucked it away, and rode off, mission accomplished.

For a while, Mankins moaned in misery, beyond human help, then at last all was still.

The emigrants buried him in a shallow grave on the trail, drove the wagons over it to disguise the spot and kept going.

Holmes Gets Hangman's Noose

Herman Webster Mudgett (1861-1896) graduated from the University of Michigan Medical School in 1884 and moved to Chicago to practice pharmacy. He also began to engage in a number of shady business, real estate, and promotional deals under the name "H. H. Holmes." Holmes was a handsome, intelligent man of great personal charm. By the time he took a job as a chemist at a Chicago area drugstore in 1888, he had already abandoned two wives and committed a variety of felonies, such as defrauding one of his in-laws. In 1890, after the proprietress of the drugstore disappeared, Holmes took over the business, selling by mail order patent medicines he had invented.

At about the same time, Holmes also began to build a "castle" of brick across the street. The castle featured soundproof bedrooms with peep holes and sliding panels. Doors locked only from the outside. It also boasted fake ceilings, secret passages, and a circular hall leading nowhere. One room had torture equipments installed. There was a room for surgery. Most curious of all were greased chutes leading from a gas chamber into vats of acid. An exceptionally roomy stove was installed in one room. Holmes changed contractors several times and shuffled the workers around frequently so that no one ever got a clear idea of the floor plan or what the building was for.

One of Holmes's partners, Ben Pitezel, took out a life-insurance policy on himself for $10,000 with Holmes as beneficiary. The plan was that Pitezel would "disappear" to Philadelphia and Holmes would produce a false corpse, identify it as Pitezel's, and share the payoff with Pitezel's family. Pitezel disappeared on schedule and Holmes collected the money. But someone tipped off the police about the scheme, and Holmes fled with the Pitezel's eldest daughter. Tell-

The handsome and charming Holmes preyed on the people of Chicago during the 1890's. He is widely known and regarded as the first serial killer in American History.

ing Mrs. Pitezel that her husband was hiding in a nearby city, Holmes convinced her to follow him, and for months the trio moved separately and together around the United States and Canada, taking the four other Pitezel children with them.

During the group's wanderings Ben Pitezel's body was discovered in Chicago and Holmes was charged with murder. Meanwhile, Holmes had dispatched three of the five Pitezel children and hid their bodies. When the police searched the Holmes castle they discovered two sheet-iron tanks containing human bones and a large furnace, believed to be a crematory.

Aided by Mrs. Pitezel, the police finally captured Holmes/Mudgett. He was tried, convicted and

executed for the murders of Ben Pitezel and the three children.

Holmes used his hours in prison by writing a book that explained his innocence. Readers did not believe him. He attempted to defend himself but failed miserably. He was convicted of first degree murder of Henry Pitezel on November 4, 1895. The Philadelphia Inquirer printed a long confession in which Holmes claimed he was innocent, but hopelessly entangled in some type of urge to kill that rendered him only a tool. In his own words, he was born with the Evil One as a sponsor and helpless. "I was born with an urge to kill."

A rare photograph of the Murder Castle as it looked in the mid-1890's.
Holmes used the second and third floors as his living quarters and for the infamous "guest rooms".
Courtesy of Chicago Historical Society

Pioneer Patrick Quinlan
Explored The Red River, Ottertail City and More!

On December 26, 1903, pioneer Patrick Quinlan, the first white settler in Burlington Township, of Becker County, Minnesota, wrote: "I was born in Canada close to the village of Norwood on the 15th day of February, 1836. Father and mother were Irish. I worked on father's farm until I started west. I arrived in St. Paul in May of 1854. St. Paul was a very small village at that time. I stayed one night, took the steam boat to St. Anthony the next day and came to Sauk Rapids. No Minneapolis or St. Cloud existed.

"I started for Long Prairie and it was the Winnebago Agency at that time. The first man I worked for lived down below Big Lake and he was a new settler by the name of Foiles. I worked for two months and a half at twenty dollars per month and I never got my pay. He accidentally shot himself and his wife promised to pay me, but I never troubled her about the money. It was a bad start, however, as I lost a good deal of my wages afterwards. For three or four years before the war, when a man got his money, it was very often no good. No-one would accept it. Every man that was doing any business had what was called a bank detector. I worked for a man called Bonfield, who lived at Rice Lake near St. Anthony. He was in the lumber business and paid me a hundred and twenty dollars and the money was no good.

"In the year 1859 a man on his way to the Red River offered me twelve dollars a month if I would go and help him through his work and work for him through the winter, which I did, commencing the spring of 1860. I got a chance to work on the first steamboat as watchman on the Red River owned by Mr. Burbank of St. Cloud. The boat was built by Anson Northrop at Georgetown and after working on the boat I got tired of the business and a man offered me twenty dollars a month to go with a party headed out to Blackfoot country. They were going to trade for horses so I started with them in a party of eight. After traveling some days we found ourselves among the buffalo. I never saw so many. We struck the Blackfoot trail close to Bear Paw Mountains and followed the trail northwest for four days before we over took the Indians. During the time we were following the Indian trail we saw many buffalo that the Indians had killed and left without taking any part of them.

"When I came the nearest settlers were at Rush Lake. Otter Tail City was the nearest store. When I came into the place I paid two dollars and twenty-five cents a bushel for ten bushels of potatoes at Otter Tail City. Flour was seven dollars a sack, pork thirty-five cents a pound. During the first winter I had to carry flour, pork and other supplies on my back from Otter Tail City. It was impossible to go with oxen in the snow, which was so deep, and no road. The first summer I was there I put up 30 tons of hay and thought I could sell it to the parties who were hauling supplies to White Earth for the Indians

who had been removed there by the government. But as soon as cold weather set in they hauled all the supplies around by Leech Lake.

"I started from Otter Tail City one day about the middle of February on Indian snowshoes. I had eighty pounds of flour and other stuff on my back. Night overtook me not far from where Perham now stands. It was cloudy and dark and I got lost. After wandering about for a long time I came to the Otter Tail river about a mile before the crossing, then I knew where I was. There was an open space in the ice so I had to step into the water. The space was not very wide and the water only a little above my knees. The night was not cold and I traveled about a mile and finding myself pretty tired, stopped and rested. When I started out again I discovered that I was unable to carry my pack so I had to leave it until the next day. I arrived home after midnight....a very tired man!

"There were a lot of ducks, chickens and other game at that time and I shot a large bear. When I first saw her, she had a large cub with her and I did not have my gun with me. I went home and got the gun which was loaded with shot and I added a bullet to each barrel and started after her. Hunting around for a time in the brush I heard her run but I could not see her. She went west toward the river and I took a short cut, but when I arrived I didn't know if she was ahead or behind me. I walked very carefully for some time and was surprised to see her standing on her hind feet about 6 feet from me.

"I aimed at her chest and pulled the trigger.... the gun did not go off! It seemed to scare her and she got down and walked sideways on all four feet. She turned toward me. I pulled the other trigger, the gun went off and she fell. I loaded the barrel again and went to her. She was dead. That same week I shot

two wildcat, some mink and one fox. After living there four years and losing my claim I moved to White Earth. I found a claim suited to me north of Buffalo River. I took land in my wife's name and we are still living on the same land. My health has been very poor and I do not expect to get rich, but I am content.

"Farewell, my true friends, for I do not think it best to trouble you any more."
Yours truly,
P. Quinlan

(Patrick Quinlan died at his home near Richmond on March, 10, 1905.)

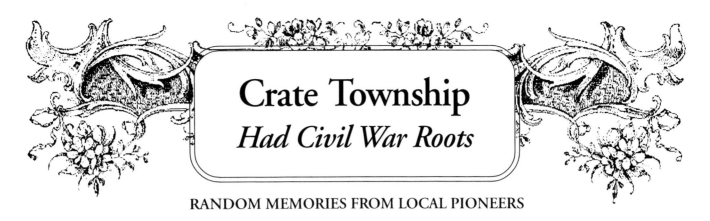

Crate Township
Had Civil War Roots

RANDOM MEMORIES FROM LOCAL PIONEERS

Crate Beasley cut a wide swath in pioneer history, not the least of which was having a township named after him. Before settling down, he fought in the Civil War and marched with General Sherman all the way to the sea. He was intensely interested in community affairs, proving it by playing the flute to the accompaniment on the piano of his daughter Flossie, who also yodeled.

Although Crate and his fellow pioneer neighbors got together for fun, there were times after disasters that getting together kept them going. Storms, blizzards and fire were the big three. It was not unusual for a blizzard to blow three or four days. One winter cattle and horses were trapped in a barn for three days without food or water. The Beasely boys finally cut a hole in the roof...then were afraid to go down among the crazed animals. They tossed feed down until the animals quieted.

Prairie fires were even more dreaded than storms. They roared across the land with a mile front, sometimes. They left nothing behind but ashes. One pioneer family plowed four wide furrows around a patch of thistles they were trying to eradicate. A stiff wind talked the fire into jumping the fire break. It was then that they discovered the ground they were standing on was peat. After burning all winter the year of 1827 it was still so hot in the spring that Anton Fritz was able to light his pipe at the edge of a bog.

Mrs. John Johnson of New London, Minnesota, explained the use of buffalo rings to her children in the event one of them might get caught in a fire. In prairie country with a sea of tall grass a mother buffalo tramps down the grass 'round and round' until she has a large circle. The tall grass keeps the calves from getting lost and predators from spotting them so easy. When the pair moves on after a few days, buffalo bulls use the rings to display their strength by ramming their horns into the sod until it is black earth. With care, these rings make a small fire hard to spot. They also have been used to escape a fire.

A cyclone in 1911 got the attention of everyone for miles. Somehow, it seemed to have a grudge against rural school houses in that part of Crate Township and took out three. It leveled District 69, spreading it over fields a half-mile away. Then it moved on to wipe out District 60 before this wild fiasco came to a stop by flattening District 3. A number of barns, including Richard Korn's new one, houses and fields also proved to be in the way.

The Walter Reiners, immigrants from East Frieland, Germany, bought 160 acres. He married Anke Valentine and they moved to a granary-barn combination house for a time. It was on May 3, 1892, that Walter had the chilling experience of running down a muddy road in his long johns and bare feet. He was hot on the heals of grain sacks blowing here and there, tumbling wildly on the open prairie. Grain sacks were a scarce commodity. He had to catch them! The Reiners had ten children. He knitted socks every night while his wife worked on making underwear. Richard died on December 3, 1943, peacefully in his rocking chair.

Mr. and Mrs. Crate Beasley

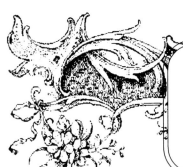

Run Into A Blizzard....Or Burn!

Ole Troovien jerked from deep slumber to sit up, wide awake. A raging storm shook the heavy logs of his cabin like a pup with a shoe. Blizzards on these South Dakota prairies howled for days unchecked. Ole knew that sound. Then he smelled smoke. "Guri! Guri!" he called, but she was already up. Ole grabbed Kristi, who was four. Guri got ten-month-old Pedre. Together they lunged toward the single door.

Clear of the fire they stopped to collect their wits. It was frigid in a bank of snow up to their waists. A stiff wind made even standing difficult. Their tracks were already gone. They watched flames reaching for the sky. Guri wished with all of her heart that she hadn't stored clothes to be washed in the loft where she couldn't grab them now.

Ole watched with a sinking heart. His brother Nels' cabin was the closest, a very long mile away. A fine powder of snow battered them from all directions making breathing nearly impossible. The high pitched howl of the wind told Ole it had not reached its zenith yet. It would get worse and colder. It was hours away from being blown out.

Ole clutched his shivering little daughter closer, heading in what he hoped to be the direction of the stable. His feet guided the way. If they stayed on the path footing was solid. A step to either side sent him sprawling into deep snow. Pedre, screaming in terror, was hard for Guri to hold with arms numbed with cold. Not letting himself think, Ole plowed ahead. He must have missed the stable, buried deep in drifts. His foot hit something solid. Setting Kristi down, he started to dig with hands that did not feel.

A door, he was down to the top of a door so banked with snow it may as well been nailed shut. In the back of the stable was a small square opening they pushed hay through into the loft. The wind made trying to talk to Guri a lost cause. Ole found the door, cleared the snow away, yanked it open and pushed his family through.

It was as frigid inside the loft as outside, but they were out of the wind. They could see through the cracks the reluctant dawning of a new day. How long could Guri and the children endure this intense unrelenting cold? Ole knew he had to try something. As scantily clad as he was, could he hope to make it to Nel's? He had to try!

Planting a kiss so cold it went unfelt on each cheek, Ole crawled out into the weather. Guri waved at her brave young husband for what she was sure the last time. None of them were going to make it. In the barn below the few heads of livestock trying to stomp life into themselves sounded like a big herd. Throwing heads this way and that made chains rattle as if straight from the depths of hell. They were thirsty. Sobs shook Guri, sure that her Ole would be found next spring after the snow melted.

Ole stood for a minute. Usually when he went to Nels' place he faced head on into the wind. It was battering him from the northeast now, which meant it was blasting him on the side. He would have to go straight, quartering the wind. If his legs held out he had a chance. Four hours had passed since Ole disappeared into the storm. For Guri time stopped.

Due to exhaustion or cold, Guri slept. It was a sound alien to the storm that brought her awake. Something scraping outside on the wall...or was it the cattle below? Then the little door pried open and a distraught Ole looked in. Icicles fringed his beard. He was plastered with snow. Nels and his brother-in-law, Hans Ligre, were with him. The way Ole managed to figure out directions worked. He walked almost straight to his brother's cabin, where his sister and her family also lived. Immediately, they gathered warm clothing and blankets. The three men took apart a bob sled, using only front runners which

would be easy to pull. Nels grabbed an armful of willow twigs and branches to push into the snow at intervals to guide them back. It was still drifting. Upon reaching the stable the men lost no time. Wrapping Guri and the children in blankets they put them on the sleigh. When they went past the cabin, Guri looked at the blackened spot in the snow. It still smoldered.

During the following two months, until spring, three families made their home with the Nels Troovien family. Ten people lived in this 15 by 18 foot cabin. As soon as the snow melted, the entire colony of pioneers helped Ole cut and haul logs. After spring work was done the new cabin was constructed, a few feet at a time, a bit bigger than the one that burned down.

Ole never forgot that helpless devastating feeling of not even knowing where his own stable was, or how to get in it, with his freezing family depending upon him for life. Right after thanking their Maker they moved in. After that, Ole busied himself with attaching a strong cord from his doorway to the stable.

THE BIG SHOW!
THE MASTODON OF THE AGE!
WILL EXHIBIT IN

RED WING,
MONDAY, JULY 29, 1867.

HAIGHT & CHAMBERS' COLLOSSAL CIRCUS AND MENAGERIE!

An advertisement from the Goodhue County Republican

Life and Death of Ol' Mother Feather Legs

When the body of Ol' Mother Feather Legs was found face down in the mud, apparently murdered while drawing water, the cowboys who had known her mourned. She chewed, smoked a pipe, cursed like a blue mule and could drink anything her customers did. She understood them. Her choice of clothes gained her the name she got hung with. She was in her forties, older than most women in her profession. Her under pants were full legged, adorned with several layers of lace at the knees. When she rode hell bent for leather across the prairie, long red hair flying and lace ruffles fluttering wildly in the wind, one cowboy was inspired to drawl "Them there drawers makes the old girl look like a feather legged chicken in a high wind." The moniker stuck.

When Ol' Mother Feather Legs landed in Wyoming in 1876 she lost no time slamming together a sod dugout on the trail between Cheyenne and the Black Hills. Here, she supplied cheap whiskey, sex, and gambling. Outlaws soon found the spot to be just right to hide out in after robbing a stage. Being shrewd, Ol' Mother saw the need for someplace the crooks could leave the loot they lifted until they wanted it, and became their bank, of sorts, a detail that more than likely had something to do with her demise.

A sleazy lout called "Dangerous Dick Davis" moved in with her, claiming to be a trapper but managing to spend long hours around her place. After another pioneer woman found Mother Feather Legs in the mud, the absence of Dangerous Dick was noticed, as well as the print of his moccasins in the mud at the spring. Some time later, he was discovered back in his old stamping ground in the swamp land of Louisiana. Before he was lynched, he admitted killing Mother Feather Legs, whose real name was Mrs. Charlotte Shepard. According to Davis, she

had been an active member of a gang of cutthroats ranging around Louisiana after the Civil War. After her gangster sons had been caught and hung she high-tailed it north.

Ol' Mother Feather Legs was buried close to where she was found. Then, years later, on May 17, 1964, Deadwood Police Chief Lee Karas drove a stagecoach up the Cheyenne Hills trail to the sagebrush covered pastures of Rawhide where a 3,500-pound stone of red granite marker was dedicated to the memory of colorful Ol' Mother Feather Legs. A colorful pair of bloomers with a lace trim was draped over the stone. The bloomers disappeared immediately following the ceremony.

In 1990, spirited citizens armed with a proclamation from the governor, retrieved the drawers, taking them off a girl in a bar who was wearing them.

Today the famous pantalets, or a close imitation thereof, can be seen on display at the Stagecoach Museum in Lusk, Wyoming.

Teddy Tender Foot

Even though Teddy was welcome in every state of the union as well as other countries, he seemed to prefer the jagged skyline of South Dakota Territory. There was a rough and ready, hell-for-leather kind of living there that he envied. There, few real men died in bed. Wild Bill Hickock slept with his gun. An eastern medic opined that what ailed Teddy would not be healed by anything that came in the shape of a pill. A pallid complexion, weak watery blue eyes behind thick bottle-bottom spectacles and prominent front teeth did nothing to suggest their owner take up a stressful kind of life. However, that's exactly what happened.

Nothing amused hard riding, born in the saddle cowboys more than having an eastern tender foot in their midst. Practical jokes, no matter how mean, were a regular diet on the streets of Deadwood as well in other frontier towns and out on the range. Teddy exactly fit the bill. He rode a rather nondescript brown horse not unlike a dozen others. One day when he was occupied elsewhere, pranksters took off the saddle and put it on another look-alike no cowboy had been able to fork for more than a few back breaking, teeth jarring jumps, a renowned bucker.

When Teddy came back to mount his horse, he saw nothing wrong. He gave the pokes leaning on the rail a wave and was well down main street when the bucker boiled over. Like the "Strawberry Roan", it went up toward the east and came down toward the west at least a half-dozen times. It stopped short after a run, skidding both front feet. It sun fished and crow hopped, plain mean clear through.

By now Teddy knew he had been had. He may not have been an example of what every young man should strive to look like, but he was tough. He hung on like a sand burr.

After his horse was winded he rode up to the rail still hung with cowboys, for the most part pretty quiet now. "It's not good manners to ride another man's horse, so I'll take mine now, please." A few days later a driver at the bar belittled Teddy. He invited the man outside behind the Cattleman's Hotel, where Teddy proceeded to make the man wish he had stayed in bed that morning. Most people didn't know Teddy could box like that.

One of the jokes spun by those who lived in this sweltering land was about a man who lived in one of the hottest spots in a hot state but unlike many, never complained. When he died and it was assumed he went to hell, an acquaintance said, I bet that'll be hot enough for him. Then the man who had been in a hell a few days called up to one of his friends, "Hey, send me down a couple of blankets. I'm freezing to death." Teddy Roosevelt was a pro at telling jokes, being able to dish it out as well as take it on the chin.

The buffalo are protected in the Theodore Roosevelt National Memorial Park. Roosevelt in 1885 reported his feelings this way about the needless slaughter: "..the extermination of the buffalo has been a veritable tragedy of the animal world... no sight is more common on the plains than that of a bleached buffalo skull; and their countless numbers attest the abundance of the animal at a time not so very long past..."

How the Dakotans Fought Off Rustlers

Christina Matson Halvorsen does not remember the storm at sea that made everyone but her seasick. She was three years old when her family left Sweden to find a better new land. They chose a farm near Vermillion, South Dakota. She had two brothers, Olin and Matt.

In the spring of 1889, Christina, Olin, and Matt homesteaded in Lyman County, where they became involved in the struggle between the western lawless element and law-abiding homesteaders.

At this time, Chamberlain, South Dakota, was a small town, thirty miles north of a place called Phelps Island, owned by Frank Phelps, who was top dog in a fearless band of outlaws, who used his island as a sanctuary. The aim of the outlaws was to keep the bottom land west of the river free of settlers to keep the outlet open for moving stolen stock. They boasted they would drive homesteaders out or let them lay where they landed if they would not go.

Christina was able to get prime acreage directly opposite the Phelps spread, because no one else wanted to be that close. Before moving, Christina and Matt had taken a twelve-year-old boy, George McDonald, from an orphanage to help with light chores. It was not long before Matt and Christina knew something odd was going on at the Phelps'. When the rustlers realized they were being watched they decided that Christina and Matt must be removed.

Christina was surprised when a hand from Phelps came to borrow a few cupfuls of sugar. A week later he returned it. It was put in the sugar bowl and George became violently ill. Christine knew it had been poisoned. They were aiming to kill all of them. Their cattle dog was poisoned, but Christina realized she was the one they really wanted.

On May 20, 1893, Christina and Matt received a letter from Olin. As Matt sat down in the doorway in the twilight to read it, a shot rang out and Matt fell over backward. At first Christine thought George had been hit. Only when the boy screamed did she realize that Matt had been killed.

Christina saw the figure of a man and recognized him as Henry Schroeder, a Phelps henchman. She tried to get out a window to go to a neighbors but heard the click of a trigger and speedily got back in. When daylight dawned she could see that her hair, a dark brown, now had white streaks through it. George ran for the nearest neighbor. Help finally arrived. Lyman County was unorganized at that time and attached to Brule County, with Chamberlain as the county seat.

Schroeder made no effort to escape and was arrested, along with Phelps, who had bribed Schroeder to kill both Christina and Matt. The case was tried twice in Lyman County, but because of the strong feeling in favor of the Matsons a new trial was granted and took place in Alexandria, county seat of Hanson County.

The Matsons obtained the best legal counsel in the Northwest. Dick Haney, Judge of the Fourth Judicial Circuit, presided over the trial. During the two years the case lasted the court room was packed. Great interest was manifested throughout the Northwest because of the problems cattle rustling had presented. The case was bitterly contested. Phelps and Schroeder were desperately fighting for their lives; on the other hand, the Matsons were determined that all who had been implicated should be punished to the full extent of the law. Following guilty verdicts, Judge Haney sentenced Schroeder to life imprisonment and hard labor at the Sioux Falls penitentiary, where he died in 1902. Phelps, who was sentenced to hang, died a few weeks after the trial. With this the ring of rustlers that had poisoned the territory for so long was broken up.

In 1897, Christina sold the ranch and went into business with her brother, Olin. In the spring of 1904 Christina Matson and Halvor Halverson were married. They had one daughter, Helen. Christina, who passed away at her home in Kimball in January 1925, had come a long way from her home in Sweden.

Family On The Move
A First Person Dakota Diary

John Sutherland drowned in the 1863 flood waters. He left a widow and five children. He was my uncle. I am Eliza Jordon and I was born October 7th, 1854, near Batavia in Kane County, Illinois. I was a year old when my parents, Peter and Isabel Jordan, operated a saw mill behind their house. Upon hearing about Uncle John's needy family they made them a visit.

Father took the whole thing on. It looked like it would be easier to move his family there, too. Having decided this, he went into Brookley Bottom and put up hay to be used for his cattle. There were 13 people in that small house but I don't recall thinking it was crowded. Since we moved early in the fall father had to bring cords of wood, lots of food, and winter clothes. This all had to be enough to do us at least two years. This all went into a porch off the kitchen.

I got scared silly on my birthday, October 7, 1863. Things had gone fairly well until then. I woke up that night from my upstairs bedroom to find the house was on fire. Flames were licking their way up the studdings but I found the railing on the stairs in all the smoke. I couldn't breathe or see. I missed a step and fell to the bottom. I wasn't hurt too bad. Somebody grabbed my arm and shoved me out in the snow. It was cold but I could see to breathe. We were all shivering in night clothes while we watched our house burn. The smoke made my eyes water so much nobody knew I was crying.

Moe Nelson lived about a mile away and was bound to take us home with him. He was a young unmarried man who lived with his folks in a two-room house, without a door between. There was a sort of curtain. We kids all had to go to bed until they found clothes for us. Older folks were running all over finding any size of clothes and material, and most people brought us something. A few came just to look.

Father worked all the time, selling our stock, trying to rent a house. It had to be near here to stay close to the hay he put up. Ma and me felt funny when Pa bought the Wiseman's house and furniture in it. We tried not to think about how Indians came and killed all their children in this house. The father and mother never went back into that house. Maybe we shouldn't either. Pa never listened. Poor mother hardly ever slept for fear of the Indians. If cattle rubbed on our house at night she almost died. Pa didn't talk much, but he was always checkin'. Deep snow that winter took care of that worry.

In 1864 farming in the Dakota's boomed. Vermilion was laid out by Nelson Miller on his land in 1860. Homesteads near town went fast. Closer to stores, schools, and churches. Most important was protection. People from the Nebraska side swarmed to Vermilion. A soldier wanted to sell the land pa bought. A fair sized log house was on the property. Pa took it down and floated the logs down the river to use for building our house. The school was a subscription one and the meeting was in Aaron Carpenter's house on our homestead during the summer of 1864.

Captain Nelson Miller really impressed me. He came in uniform to talk to father. I peeked around a corner of the house. They were talking about school. Sounded like he had 6 children all school age. I heard pa say he could furnish the logs and teams. Captain Miller said that would be fine, then he would provide soldiers to do the work.

It was Grandmother Sutherland's claim where we got the logs. Except for sodding the roof it was done in one day. We didn't know it then, but this was the first school in South Dakota, taught by a

soldier by the name of "Amos Shaw". He also laid out the town sites of Brookings and Sioux Falls.

Sioux Falls is where we went if we just had to. One time when Pa came home he surprised ma with a set of hand carved chairs of hickory wood with woven bark seats. Time passed and we grew up. I taught school in Vermilion, later filing on a claim south of Mitchell. On April 14, 1879, Charles Miner took land in Beadle County. He was working on his claim one day when a messenger told him his father had died. He left for Vermilion to help with things and be with his mother. He stayed around for several months while he did small jobs. Now, the Baums, mother and Ed, were his first neighbors.

Charles borrowed a team in September of 1880 from James Bishop. He left a boy trapper, Frank Booth, in charge of his place. Each week found the snow a little deeper. Nobody could get to Huron. We worked for our wedding, planned for December 1, at mother's, in 1880. She had been a widow for several years. We had 7 days of hard driving. I'll never forget those awful days. We reached our claim December 9. I got a look at our first home. The cabin was of limestone. It had thick walls, deep window seats and a built in bookcase. On December 10th we sewed up carpet strips I had put together for our rug. The walls were smooth and plastered, the only lumber being in the door. I was delighted! When this was done the room looked bright and cheerful. I have never had a room I liked as much. Mrs. James Bishop was my first guest.

Snow was relentless. It got deeper and deeper with the narrow roads all closed. For the first months we had plenty. Charles shot antelope and prairie chickens for meat. Charles had raised a flock of chickens and we had one for dinner every Sunday. I was running out of flour. We heard that a neighbor had brought groceries from Huron, 12 snowy miles away across a river on a railroad open bridge. Charles and Mr. Bishop made the trip on homemade snow shoes made from willow branches, gunny sack, and clothesline. One neighbor, the Baums, had raised some wheat. Charles bought 2 pounds. It wasn't enough to grind and make bread, so I boiled it and we ate it that way.

The Federal Court at Yankton summoned Charles to be a witness at the Cameron trial. He had to hurry before spring of 1881 breakup. He walked

as far as Brigg's place, near Forestburg. He was tired of walking and bought a pony. We named him Bolivar. He was a great horse for many years. His weight broke through the ice so we made a hand sled and rigged a harness, a gunny sack for a collar and back boards, ropes for lines. Going was better then and he reached Yankton without breaking through again.

Then the big thaw came. Court was adjourned. Vermilion nearly drifted away. Mecklin, where Charles' sister lived, washed away when the snow started to melt. Charles and six other men went to help rescue her, as well as some others marooned on the top of a grain elevator, where they had been for a week. Charles came home as soon as he could. Water was all around and he couldn't ride the pony. It was tired and slow. They had to swim part of the way and the pony was not a good swimmer. Unless Charles swam ahead he refused to get in the stream. Charles stripped, rolled his clothes on a bundle and tied them to Bolivar's head and they swam acrossed. On the other side he put them on again. It was cold.

The water was all around our house on the claim. It came higher and higher until I had to leave. The Bishop's came in a canoe to rescue me. A hole was burned in one end so we all had to set in the other end. They helped move our stuff to the top of a hill. They begged me to come along but I was afraid of that canoe. I spent two days and two nights on the top of that hill with my furniture and stock. I had two calves to feed. I took hay out of the tick to feed the cows. Bishop came back and said I had to go with him. So I went.

In all this time I had not heard from my husband. I was anxious. One day Bishop brought a paper saying how bad it was around Vermilion and Yankton. It said Charles Miner had left with a yawl and six men to rescue people at Mecklin and that he hasn't been heard from since. It is believed that his party drowned. I knew how clever Charles was in water. Many days went by with no word but I still believed him alive. Time seemed to stand still. Long days and longer nights. One day Mr. Bishop brought

me a whole bunch of mail! Most was letters from Charles. The next day he and Bolivar jogged home.

What a relief! That summer we had good crops and in September, 1881 our son, Nelson, was born.

Eliza and Charles Minor had five children: Nelson, James, Grace and two daughters who died as babies. Charles was born in the adobe house which was torn down in 1891. Isabel and Ruth were born after the family had moved to the frame house. Now it stands on the home place, south of Pearl Creek.

They lived on this claim for the rest of their lives. They developed it into a stock farm. When they were 65 they turned the farm over to their three sons. Winters were spent in California. In 1923 they bought a home in Huron, South Dakota. That's where they spent the rest of their lives.

Charles died June 15, 1927, at the age of 72, Eliza, and her sister Grace Jordon stayed in Huron. A stroke crippled Eliza and she spent the last ten years of her life in bed. Release for her came on January 3, 1953, one year short of the century mark.

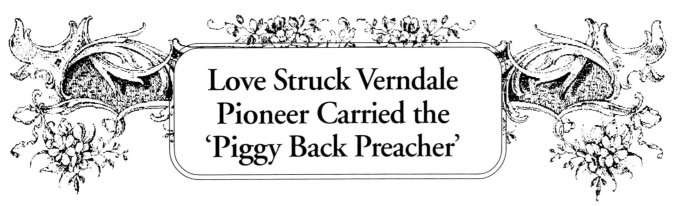

Love Struck Verndale Pioneer Carried the 'Piggy Back Preacher'

If Sanderson had more than a last name, no one knew it. In 1878, he settled on what was virgin prairie on a spot that now hosts Osage, Minnesota. There were still many square miles of prairie to be had for any pioneer brave enough to take the plunge. After making this major decision, Sanderson knew that in order to get past the first few requirements to prove-up, he needed a wife.

The land Sanderson chose for himself lay 45 miles from Verndale, Minnesota, was parcel number one along the banks of Wing River. On parcel three, lived a Mr. Sloan, who had settled up a few years earlier, and next to him lay parcel two. Both properties lay on what was to be later known as "The Wheat Trail". To his credit, Sanderson also "happened" to notice that among the pioneers who lived in a half-dozen cabins in the community was an efficient girl he guessed would be in her middle teen years. While he courted her, he hired out for odd jobs because he needed money.

Jake Graba turned his place into a halfway stop. He settled on Shell River where Shell City soon sprung up. The land from Shell City to Verndale switched back and forth from deep timber to miles of swamp. Rivers that had to be crossed were Wing River, Leaf River, Hay Creek, Red Eye, and Cat Creek twice. Traffic on the trail increased to where Graba's place was not large enough. He could give worn out teams a dry stall and their drivers a warm bed only by enforcing a few laws of his own making. Graba settled this by notifying the last driver in that he would instantly be disaccommodated should another tired rig and driver seeking food and rest show up. Mr. Sloan knew this to be a fact as he had been unceremoniously been kicked out with his team in the middle of the night in January. It had been a chance to get dry, eat, and with as many as four to a bed at $3 a head, getting warm was not a problem.

As parcels were taken, Shell City grew from a halfway house to a metropolis that boasted a population of 100. It had two mills, two blacksmith shops, hotels and stores. Clam shells in abundance showing up along the river spawned a clam shell button factory that thrived. A mill owned by Mose Stewart in Verndale came along about the same time, in 1911. Wheat that stirred the heart of a poet undulated forth and back in every breeze like an ocean of golden color. Each acre was producing 35 or 40 bushels an acre on this new land.

While history was being made in the fields, Sanderson was making hay with the settler's daughter. While Sanderson's goal to acquire a fine wife was accomplished, Shell City's prospects for a future grew slim. New land produced big-time for a few years, then unless nutrients were added, the virgin land petered out and yields dropped. Shell City also dropped in importance as the railroad was coming in eleven miles to the south to Wadena, or north to Park Rapids.

The apple of Sanderson's eye agreed to become his wife, but only if a bona fide man of the cloth pronounced them man and wife. Finally, by following Wing River through what seemed to be bottomless sloughs miles across and fording several rivers, Sanderson made his way to the nearest Sky Pilot's house. Yes, the cleric who lived there would go with him. They started back as soon as Sanderson was rested.

Preacher and Sanderson packed as many provisions as each could carry and started out. The first miles north of Verndale were uneventful. Then they came to the Wing River, flooded out of its banks, and it became plain that the preacher's long suit was not fording rivers or wading sloughs. The journey came to an end days later than Sanderson had planned, with him so bushed he could scarcely get up the stoop. He'd had to carry the preacher piggy back, well above the waterline, for miles and miles.

Ghost Town: *Dilemma At White Rock*

Meet a town which, not unlike her human counterparts, arose from the dust, boomed a few years, then without a whimper returned from whence she came. One-hundred and sixty years in history is but a moment in the scheme of time, for it can spell out two lifetimes or eight generations. We invariably hone in on environment to meet our needs, taking nature from wilderness to bustling activity and industry, then back to wilderness when we are attracted elsewhere.

White Rock, which was incorporated in 1884, is located on the west bank of Bois de Sioux River, 100 feet from Minnesota and a mile south of North Dakota. According to the Indians, a white rock 5 feet high and 18 feet long gave White Rock its name. The Indians prized it and took care of it, until white businessman S.E. Oscarson blew it to smithereens on May 20, 1899, in order to make room for two elevators. When the Sisseton Indian Reservation opened in 1892, it was like a shot in the arm for White Rock.

White Rock took on life as surreptitiously as toad stools appear after a warm spring rain, a rainbow after a storm, with the energy of the proverbial bat out of hell. Within the next few years streets were laid out, foundations poured, and committees elected to put together a city. Public servants were hired, job descriptions passed out.

S. E. Oscarson's new store was 140 feet by 50 feet, boasting to be the biggest store under one roof between Fargo and the Twin Cities. He threw a grand opening party, with people attending from miles away. Popular Brown's Orchestra played to as many as 70 couples on the floor at one time. Farmers were shipping a million bushels or forty box car loads of grain. When elevators bulged, golden piles of bounty waited on the ground. Finding employment was a breeze, even up to 100 hobos who slept under the railroad bridge had work, a cupboard, and drank from Porcelain cups.

A population of 600 supported seven grain elevators, two feed mills, three blacksmith shops, two livery stables, five farm implements, two harness shops, two banks, one newspaper, two doctors, three

Carrie Lindblom

lawyers, two land offices, one creamery, six general stores, two hardware, two drug, two confectionery, one furniture, one undertaker, two shoe shops, three hotels, two lumber yards, steam fitting shop, one dentist, two restaurants, a social hall and four saloons.

To keep spirits high, there was a sporty orchestra and a baseball team, sometimes called "The White Rock 9." Their biggest competitor was the Wheaten team. In one game, when the score was 0 to 6 in favor of White Rock at the end of the sixth inning, the visitors, who hadn't gotten a man as far first base, got mad, picked up their balls and bats, and went home.

Thriving businesses in 1903 were able to click a switch instead of lighting a lamp with a glow of a 15 watt bulb. Cartwright Implement devised a large gas plant that generated votalite gas in their building from the far end of main street. It was piped to all business places at the cost of 2 1/2 cents per cubic foot. When a heavily loaded cart broke through bending a gas main, after a period of going back to lamps, the company built a bigger storage tank with lights equal to 75 watt bulbs. In 1908, when a car back fired, burning a block of the town down, several saloons were victims. In one instance, when slot

machines were moved to the middle of a street for safety, John Olson kept on playing the piano. In the 1930's, during the Great Depression, one of the White Rock's banks, managed by a man named "Powell," was the only lending institution in the county that did not close its doors.

White Rock had a whimsical side as well. A livery stable boasted of having the only team in town who could make it to Wheaten and back, some 80 miles, in the same day. A birth announcement sent out by the Still family read, "On January 17, 1910, a boy of standard weight, exceptional quality, was born." When Martin Olson bet Miss Eva Lind three lots in White Rock she could get married by 4:00 p.m. the same day, she beat it down to tell her boyfriend, Bert See. They took off pronto for Wheaten, and by four o'clock were in a union never to be put asunder. Hans Thompson's enterprise, "La Grande Hotel," enjoyed steam heat for $2 a night. Carrie Nation, all six feet of her, got her destinations mixed up and quite by mistake landed in White Rock. Since they were still dry at that point here, she had no need to unpack her hatchets. The first car tootled down main street in 1911.

White Rock, alias Virginia City, had its murders, robbing, and saloon brawls. Big Louie Halvorson was 6 feet and 4 inches tall at 250 pounds. He was not only big, he was mean, with a hair-trigger temper. On November 17, 1899, two hunters came in to warm up and get a drink while he was mopping up the floor, not knowing that they were expected to also buy Big Louie a drink. He roughed them up and threw them into the middle of the street. Two hours later they came back and shot him. At 3:15 a.m. on July 7, 1904, vandals broke into Oscarson's General Store. Somehow, they set off an explosion that went off minutes after they left. The Marshal caught them in an orchard. They refused to talk about the money. When officers returned to the orchard, their attention was drawn to a patch of grass deader than the rest. When they dug it up there was the cash!

Carrie Vanderhoef Lindblom lived in White Rock the first eight years of her 101 years to date. She has a vivid memory of sliding down piles of pumpkins in the fall with other kids. She rode for hours on horseback and dispatched rattlesnakes. School was in a claim shanty, where they wrote on tables but had to bring a chair from home. It was in White Rock when she was seven that she saw her first car. The Vanderhoef family was touched by the outlaw element when their house was robbed. One night some low-life sneaked in while they were sleeping to take every dollar, as well as whatever also he wanted. He even went into the children's room and robbed little purses. For some reason Carrie no longer recalls, she was given a dime. She was so pleased that she kept it from the rest of the change by wrapping it in a square of paper. When family took

inventory, her dime was all they had left! A favorite pet was named "Fido" who followed them home from the Indian reservation. Had he known the robber? Well, he didn't bark!

Carrie married Pal Lindblom. She was a pioneer school teacher and post mistress in Aldrich, Minnesota, when wages depended upon how many stamps she sold. She retired after 24 years. Pal delivered mail on routes. He died several years ago, leaving Carrie in a snug little home on a hill, surrounded by tall sentinel trees. The walk to her home is well worn. Pal and Carrie had three children.

A Federal Highway missed White Rock to the east, the Milwaukee line to the west. With no plans for improvements, such as piped in water, doldrums set in for White Rock in the early nineties. Farmers were first to go. They were tired of having to stay over each time they brought a load of grain in. With that decision, the rug was pulled out from under every other business since farmers shopped where they sold. Every place that calls itself a city or town is susceptible to human desires, like cancerous apathy, or economic blight. Disinterested people gravitated to other situations in other places. Only sturdy foundations were left behind to prove that White Rock had ever been.

On January 8, 1913, the street lights went out, never to shine again. Phone service followed. Viola Ehless, White Rock treasurer, said before she left to winter in California that she would be coming back--to live in Minnesota. The last town meeting was held on the kitchen table of the clerk, with only herself present.

All this being said, has White Rock been forgotten? She has not! On June 24 , 1915, a crowd estimated between 3,000 and 4,000 people crowded into White Rock for a midsummer celebration. There was an Automobile Parade, and a pilot was hired to make two flights over the crowd in his Curtis bi plane. The show was a vast success.

In 1910, prosperity began separating itself from White Rock as surreptitiously as fog before morning sun. Without fan fare, people migrated to other towns situated on a railroad with water systems, taking their houses with them. White Rock put on the cloak of anonymity in 1913, edging with ever longer steps back toward wild flowers, the comforting sighing of prairie grasses.

White Rock has had its day and served its purpose. It has not lived in vain. In the words of Matilda Kendall, "It doesn't take much to diagnose a post mortem."

"We Yelled Like Hell!" - *A WWII Memoir*

I am Sgt. Bill Sandra, Yank Magazine staff correspondent and my buddies are Marine Cpl. Bernie Pitts, of Dallas and his friend Pfc. Nyndal. We had been taken prisoner by the Japs nearly a year earlier and at their hands had experienced hunger, hard beatings and sleep deprivation. There had been no news leaks, then suddenly the Japs became generous and even friendly. We each got a bottle of beer, rice, soybeans and turnips. Many prisoners gorged at the sight of so much food and were sick. None of the American prisoners had shoes or socks. The guards broke open bundles of clothing that had been saved but never given to us. An order came out that any guard who mistreated prisoners would be shot. We smiled at that order, because we were all covered with bruises and bumps from being beaten until we could no longer stand and then we were kicked.

Then on August 21, 1945, a Japanese guard came into prison to announce, "Senso shumi." That means " the war is over", but he didn't say which side had won. Then when the gates of our Yokohama prison camp on the Island of Honshu were thrown wide open and we were told we could eat all of the rice we wanted, we knew! We broke the rule of complete silence, or a shot though the head, and yelled like hell! That is, some of us did. A lot of our buddies had been beat down so many times they just sat, spirit broken, staring in one spot.

We had nothing to pack so we walked through the prison gates to the railroad station about 7 o'clock, the evening of the 30th and caught a train. It was jammed so we hung between two cars on the outside. We hung there all night. We walked down to the water front in Tokyo. We were trying to make ourselves understood to a Jap standing there when a huge B-29 came over. It was dropping stuff attached to parachutes. One dropped almost at our feet and broke open. Cigarettes, candy and cans of peaches were all over. We went kind of crazy. A driver in a Ford took us on down to the road to Tokyo. He took us on to the New Grand Hotel.

We felt self conscious as we walked into the lobby. He steered us over to the big dining room, but we told him there was too much rank in there and we didn't have time for anything fancy. So he told us to go down stairs to the 188th Parachute Infantry C.p. The G.I.'s from the 11th Airborne Division were the paratroopers and the biggest guys I had ever seen. No one paid any attention to us though we stuck out like a sore thumb. We were so thin and white. We got a glimpse of MacArthur. We had been on the rock with him. "Who will believe all this?" Prestar said and began to cry.

Survivors were loaded on barges, after the surrender at Corregidor, headed for Manila. Pitts had a shrapnel wound in the leg from a shell that killed 42 men. Prestar had been shot in the hand. They were both in a Manila Hospital, then loaded into a Cabanutuan and thrown in Bilibid Prison. They stuffed a 100 of us in a boxcar that had a capacity of 35. We walked the last 20 kilometers. We heard about the Bataan death march. We'd have never made it. After Corregidor we were nearly starved and weak.

We had a little rice twice a day. The Nips beat the hell out of anybody that lagged their stiff pace. If he didn't get up they stuck a white flag beside of him, meaning he was dead. We never knew what happened to them. We were at Cabanatuan for 5 weeks. Everybody broke out with dysentery. They fed us just enough to keep us alive. We three were sent out to the jungles to cut lumber, which saved our lives. They worked the hell out of us but we managed to pick a little fruit to eat. I am a coconut fan. There were bananas we used to sneak green and hide them until they were ripe. The Nips shot 6 who took a few bites back to camp.

On June 24, 1942, 300 American prisoners were crammed into freight cars for Palawan, to work on the airstrip. Living was terrible in all of the Jap prison camps. One-third of the men had blankets. They lived in rags. Three were beaten to death for stealing a can of meat. We stood at attention and were beat for two hours. On August of 1944 we were

shipped with 200 other prisoners to Milan and Formosa. 200 men were left in camp. In Formosa harbor a freighter was loaded on a hot August morning. 1,200 prisoners in two holds of the ship. 750 prisoners were jammed into space for 400. They had to stand up. There was one toilet bucket for all of the men in the hold. Most had dysentery. You can imagine what it was like after the first day. We couldn't breathe. We couldn't eat. I tied myself to a bulkhead. It was better than being down there.

Every morning a Nip would stick his head down the hatch to tell us to shake the one next to us. If he didn't move they'd haul him on deck and dump him over the side. Those guys were killing each other to get more room. They would strangle one another. They would put their hands around a neck and strangle. I saw one man watch his own brother get killed that way. It was a quick death.

There are 40 ships in this convoy. The convoy was attacked and we hoped we'd get hit, but we didn't. Where were plenty of Jap destroyers around covering ships. A Grumman dove down through the flack ceiling, released his bomb and shot back up, clipping a foot off a mast. It missed us by 5'. We sat in the harbor about 10 days. The weather was cold. We were so dehydrated we had quit sweating. 150 men on that trip died in the hold.

Preslar and Pitts stayed in Tokyo. It was February 15th and cold. They each got a jacket and pair of wool pants. No shoes. This was a prison transport to Moji on Kyushu Island. I was put on a train and, believe it or not, there was room to lay down. We went ashore half frozen. The two marines, Prestar and Pitts, were sent to Camp Wakanahaua near Osaka. They saw their first B 29 raid in March. They were packed in barracks. Anyone making a happy noise was shot. The raid wrecked half of Kobe and Osaka. It burned everything more than 50 feet around the camp. The next day the prisoners were transferred to Marchara in the foothills of the mountains. The camp ran parallel to a railroad in farming country. Pitts was a bugler and they put him to work. He had to learn Jap calls.

In August we heard about a new offer for peace. When prisoners arrived at the camp in Honshu each was interviewed in turn. One of the questions was "Who do you think will win this war?" Each answer was "The United States."

"Why?"

"Because the United States will be too much for you," we said. We never had the slightest doubt that the United States would win in time, Prestar said. "Not even in the Philippines after the surrender at Corregidor. I guess we all at one time or another thought that we wouldn't be alive to see it, but we knew the United States would win the war."

Lumberjack Sister Started Modern Health Insurance!

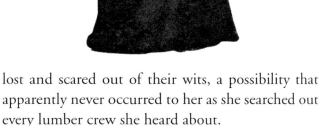

Sister Amata would have made today's hospital insurance salesmen look like pantywaists. She worked for St. Mary's hospital in Duluth, selling "health tickets" to lumbermen. Her territory included the whole north woods, or wherever lumberjacks could be found. Everyone she talked to became a customer. Seeing so many injured lumberjacks during her work in the hospital prompted Sister Amata to come up with the health ticket idea.

How wonderful it would be, she reasoned, if a lumberman's hospital bill could be paid in the event of an accident in the woods. Lumbering was hazardous work, fraught with accidents...chains broke, logs weighing tons would tumble over each other, and working around so many horses took a toll, too. There were numerous broken limbs or backs, and many lives were lost. Probably the most hazardous of all in the lumber woods was the greenhorn, responsible for more than half of the injuries to himself or those working around him.

The health ticket sold for $1.00 to $6.00 and he could use it in one of six hospitals in the area. Many a man, as he regained health, blessed Sister Amata for talking him into buying the ticket. Otherwise the hospitalization would have meant financial hardship for his family. Knowing the myriad of accidents that could happen gave Sister the zeal to keep going. Sometimes another sister, who played the violin, accompanied her, but the stamina needed limited all but Sister Amata.

The Lumberjack Sister stood well over 6' 2" and weighed more than 200 lbs. Despite her size, transportation to lumber camps was never a problem. If there wasn't a load of logs, an empty log buck, ice sled or horse headed where she wanted to go, Sister Amata expertly skimmed over land on snowshoes. The woods were full of a number of wild animals. Most lumbermen at one time or another, had become

lost and scared out of their wits, a possibility that apparently never occurred to her as she searched out every lumber crew she heard about.

A great cheer went up whenever Sister Amata entered a camp. As well as selling her tickets, she said and heard prayers, brought word from families, tucked letters to loved ones into her packet and clucked over pictures of drooling babies. If time allowed after she had her work done and before she took off for another camp, she made pies for the men. As a rule she made a bed for herself in the camp office. If the camp had no office, and not many did, she thought nothing of using the bunk house.

The sister was born Amata Macket of Karoof, Bohemia, in 1861. Her parents moved to Prairie du Chien, Wisconsin, and eventually Amata entered the St. Benedict's order in St. Joseph, Minnesota. She took her final profession to become a nun in 1885, then was transferred to St. Joseph's Hospital in Duluth.

It was sincere admiration for this unselfish, affectionate woman that prompted the lumberjacks to give Sister Amata the title "Lumberjack Sister," thus making her one of their own.

Influenza or Black Plague?

In 1918, four women played bridge late into the night. By morning three of them were dead. While this may be exaggerated, it is not too far from the truth. Flu hit almost that hard and fast.

The U.S. came in on the second round of it. Flu landed in Boston first in September of 1918 from which it spread to the troops like wild fire. The flu virus killed nearly 20,000 in October that year. Millions everywhere were infected and thousands of them died. Men on both land and sea were too sick to fight. It was said that more were killed by the flu than weapons.

China is the place where it is believed the first flu appeared. Eight million are thought to have perished in Spain. After that there was no bounds to the disaster. In 1918, when President Wilson addressed the nation, he did little to try to collar or stem the epidemic. Some felt restrictions should have been made earlier. As time went on 15 minute limits were put on public meetings or wherever people got together. As time progressed medical supplies gave out, there was a shortage of coffins, morticians, even people still strong enough to dig graves. The medical community was stripped of doctors and nurses. What with the wounded coming back from the front in droves from the war zone those in medical schools several years away from earning a diploma were pressed into service.

The flu showed no favorites, with everyone effected, including President Wilson while he was engaged in negotiating with France for the Versailles Treaty that ended World War One. The conditions in 1918 were not so far removed from the Black Death in the era of the Middle Ages.

An Emergency Hospital for Influenza Patients

Similar conditions were experienced in the Middle Ages in days of the Black Plague, when bubonic infection circled the globe. The influenza epidemic in India was devastating, with a death rate extremely high. Theories dealing with where so deadly a strain of influenza originated remain unproven. There is no doubt that it cut a wide swath wherever it went.

President Wilson

Troops parade down Woodward in 1918 wearing gauze masks in an attempt to protect themselves from the flu virus.

Pretty Boy Floyd

Charles Arthur Floyd, later to be known as "Pretty Boy Floyd," was born on February 3, 1904, in Georgia, one of seven children, but moved to a small farming community in Oklahoma, which he came to call home. His father's bootlegging business kept them in groceries.

In 1921, Floyd married sixteen-year-old Ruby Hargrove. They had one son, Jack Dempsey Floyd. Money was scarce for Charles and Ruby. He hit the hobo trail trying to find harvest jobs in Nebraska and the Dakotas. He wanted a better life for his family than he had had. However, he was not willing to wait and work much longer for it, and robbed a post office, his first crime. He got $350, all in pennies. He considered it "easy money." He was arrested on suspicion but his father gave him an alibi that saved his hide for that time. Next he robbed a Kroger Store of approximately $16,000.00.

Then he went back to Ruby. They went wild with that much money, spending it on expensive clothes and dining in expensive places. They were soon broke again. He was arrested a few months later, and when his house was searched money still in paper wrappers showed up. He was sentenced to five years in the Jefferson City Penitentiary. During this time Ruby gave birth their boy, Jackie. Within the year she divorced him. He vowed never to be locked up again. He wasn't.

It was in East Liverpool that Floyd cemented his life of crime. He was a hired gun for bootleggers and rum runners up and down the Ohio River. When he visited his folks farm he found that his father had been shot by J. Mills in an old family feud. Mills was acquitted of the crime. Floyd took his father's rifle and paid J. Mills a visit. He was never heard of again. Charles most notorious years were still ahead. He headed west to Kansas City, run by Tom Pendergast. Hired guns, murderers, all kinds of gangsters took a

Pretty Boy Floyd at Age 12.

liking to Kansas City. A madam named Beulah Baird Ash called him "Pretty Boy Floyd" and the name stuck. He hated it. It is said that Pretty Boy stayed friendly with both Ruby and Beulah all the rest of his life. He knew their husbands.

Pretty Boy went hog wild into crime for the next 12 years. He killed 10 men, robbed 30 banks. He filed a notch in his pocket watch for each one. Floyd was arrested in Akron, Ohio, in his hideout. He was tried and convicted but escaped by jumping out of a train window near Kenton, Ohio, while on his way to the penitentiary. The first person he killed was a policeman, Ralph Castner, who stopped him from robbing a bank on April 16, 1931. He was accompanied by "Billy The Killer" Miller, Beulah and her sister Rose. A clerk in a store recognized them when buying the women dresses. Police arrived while they were walking down the street, ordering them to stop. An FBI agent was gunned down in an effort to free Frank "Gentleman" Nash, a notorious underworld figure. Floyd was named Public Enemy

Charles Arthur "Pretty Boyd Floyd"

No. 1, with a $23,000 reward on his head, dead or alive. Floyd always denied being involved in this crime.

The next seven months found Floyd being hunted by all law enforcement, everywhere. This drove Floyd back to the Midwest. On October 19, 1934, he was spotted after three men dressed as hunters robbed the Tiltonsville People's Bank. Both Adam Richetti and Floyd were positively identified as two of them. Police were put on an alert all over the Midwest. That was the day before a shoot-out between the two criminals and Wellesville, Ohio, police. It ended in the capture of Richetti. Pretty Boy escaped by kidnaping a florist and stealing his car.

On October 22, 1934, things came to an end for Pretty Boy. A full force of officers were called out by Chief McDermott and Patrolman Chester Smith. Fire arms were issued but Smith preferred his 30.30 Winchester rifle. He told everyone that if they found Floyd he would be running. After all back roads had

been checked they stopped at the Conkle farm on Spruseville Road. Earlier in the day Floyd had knocked on the Conkle door posing as a hunter. Ellen Conkle bought his story and asked him in. After he had eaten, Stewart Dyke, Ellen's brother, offered to drive him to a bus station. As they were getting in the car two squad cars were seen speeding along the narrow road. Floyd jumped from the car and hid behind a corn crib. Smith recognized Floyd, who started to run. He was told to halt, he didn't, and Smith fired a shot that hit Floyd in the arm. Floyd dropped his gun and grabbed his arm, but he kept running. This time he was shot in the right shoulder.

Federal agents and local police all began to fire at the same time and Pretty Boy fell to the ground, gun at his side. Patrolman Smith checked the body. He was not dead. Floyd had another weapon in is belt. In fact, he had two Colt .45 Automatics but never got off a shot. Smith, Roth and Montgomery carried Floyd to the shade of an apple tree. He was alive when they moved him but died about 4:25. They put Floyd in the back seat of a patrol between Smith and Roth and hauled him to East Liverpool where they turned him over to the Sturgis Funeral Home.

Floyd had $120 in his pocket.

Many stories circulated about that day. It was said that Roth shot Floyd while he was sitting under an apple tree. Floyd's mother did not want his body viewed by the public. By the time Chief McCermott got her call there were thousands lined up wanting to see this famous criminal. He was shipped back to Oklahoma but in the meantime more than 10,000 people passed by the body, about 50 a minute. The mob stormed the funeral home, trampling shrubbery, ruining the lawn, breaking railings.

Pretty Boy Floyd reached his final resting place just before noon on Tuesday, October 23, 1934. His body left Liverpool in a baggage car. A year before Floyd had said to his mother when they drove past Ashings Cemetery in Sallisaw, Oklahoma, "Right here is where you can put me. I expect to go down soon with lead in me. Maybe the sooner the better. Bury me deep."

There were 20,000 people at his funeral. His head stone was chipped almost to ruin by souvenir hunters and was finally stolen. A new headstone marks his grave. A marker along the Spruceville Road between East Liverpool and Rogers, Ohio, has been erected near the Conkle farm for America to see where Public Enemy No.1 was shot.

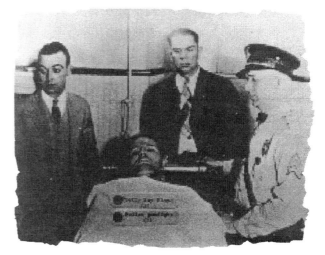

Floyd at the Sturgis Funeral Home, East Liverpool, Ohio

Jack Floyd, his son, saw his father infrequently, but said in an article for the San Francisco *Examiner* that he was a fun guy to be around. "He was like a regular dad, always bringing puppies or other presents. What I knew about him did not keep me from loving him." Ruby, agreed. She never loved anyone else as much as she did him.

Resource material for these pages are from existing old papers and microfilm on record in the Carnegie Library of East Liverpool and from records and photographs in possession of the Dawson Funeral Home.

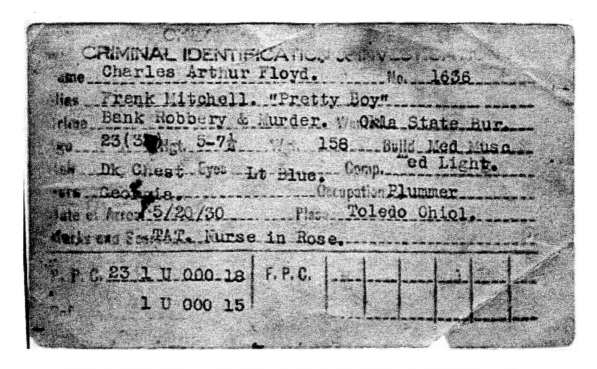

Fargo - Moorhead's Daring Darling

Both Fargo and Moorhead have claimed daring Florence Gunderson Klingensmith and she claimed both of them.

Florence began life September 3, 1904, on a farm in Oakport Township, near Moorhead, Minnesota. She had a sister and two brothers. Their father was a custodian in the local school. None of the other siblings seemed to be as carefree and devil-may-care as Florence, who went from one challenge to another. Oliver Sondrall remembers having to talk her out of trying a high ski jump from the scaffolding out near the Moorhead Country Club when he saw that she did not have bindings on her skis. "She'd have been killed!" In Moorhead, Florence was the only girl who raced through the streets on a big fast motorcycle. The Fargo *Forum* wrote that Florence got her first experience at flying on her motorcycle. Her brother George rode on the gas tank. A tire blew one time when the speedometer showed they were going 70 miles per hour. They flew.

Whatever else she did, Florence's first and last enduring love was flying. She quit high school in her junior year to work around planes. She worked at the Pantorium, a Fargo dry cleaners. She met Charles Klingensmith during those years. They were married briefly; then she wanted to be free again. She kept Charles' long name. A stop at the Fargo airport by Charles Lindbergh settled it. She opted for nothing less than a life of flying. She followed this up by joining ground electric classes at Hands on Auto and Electrical School in Fargo. There was Florence and four hundred boys. She did apprentice work at Fargo's Hector Field, where she learned planes inside and out. Florence was a fast learner and ate up her lessons and flying information. When her flight instructor needed a stunt girl on flying shows, Florence agreed to try skydiving in return for flying lessons. Once she fell unconscious when she hit the field. She still jumped again at Bismarck and Brainerd.

Florence got a lot of experience but little money, she wanted her own plane. She finally canvassed business men, promising to promote Fargo wherever she went, for enough to buy a plane. A Fargo laundry owner, William T. Lee, said, "If you are willing to risk your life I will risk some money." He did, and other business men Norman Black, William Stern, J.K. Roth Herbst, and others came up with $3,000. She bought her first plane in 1929, at Monocoupe Airplane Factory in Moline, Illinois, naming it "Miss Fargo." In June, she became the first licensed woman pilot in North Dakota and her career in flying began. She flew barnstorming fairs and worked as operations manager at Hector. She flew her first race and took fourth. Other competitions were flying loops. She flew a record 1,078 loops at Chamberlain Field in Minneapolis to take first prize.

Next Florence entered the $10,000 Frank Phillips Trophy Race in Chicago. She was the first women to sign up for that one. It was 100 mile ride, 12 laps around pylons. Florence flew a bright red Gee Bee Sportster owned by Arthur Knapp of Jackson, Michigan. The fabric covered craft's original 220 horse power engine was replaced with a souped up 670 hp motor. The overpowered engine added an element of danger, but Florence was confident. The *Chicago Daily News* quoted her as saying just before the race, "I don't know that I will win, but I do know I will place. The plane is fast enough and I can fly it." She loved that plane and seemed to understand it. She agreed to the bigger motor with some doubt.

About 4 p.m. on September 4, a day after her birthday on the 29th, she strapped herself into a plane. She was fourth from the front, ahead of four male contestants. She averaged 200 mph during the first laps. She was passing the stands when a bit of red fabric flew off the fuselage. That red BeeGee had given all it had. Florence flew out of the pattern and headed for a plowed field where it would be easier to land without endangering anyone. The crowd saw her plane flip over in the air. It nose dived to earth from 350 feet up. There was a collective gasp from the crowd as the plane smashed into the earth in a

ball of fire. Those who know said Florence died instantly. She had apparently tried to bail out because part of her chute was entangled in the fuselage.

It was determined by experts that the crash was due to structural failure, not pilot error. The mistake was replacing the the small 220 hp engine built for the plane with the huge souped-up 670. After Florence's death other women pilots were banned from entering Bendix Air Race at the 1934 Nationals. Women protested. Amelia Earhart's way of protesting was her refusal to fly Mary Pickford to Cleveland to open the air races. The women held their own races in Ohio.

Florence's body was shipped back to Moorhead for the funeral. She was treasured by other pilots, dozens of whom came from all over the country besides hundreds of friends. The funeral was held in Fargo's First Presbyterian Church. Floral tributes included one arrangement in the shape and color of her first plane, "Miss Fargo." The businessmen who had bankrolled Florence's first plane served as pallbearers. She is buried at Oakmound Cemetery, only a few miles from where she was born.

Rev. J.C, Brown, "The Flying Parson," said, "If she could speak to us now she would tell us not to lose faith in aviation because of the tragedy that ended her flying career. She would say it was not usual, but happened in the pursuit of the thrills upon which she thrived."

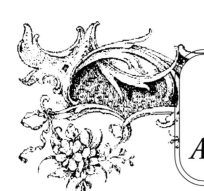

Runaway
A Memoir by Ethelyn Pearson

There is nothing much worse than seeing your four-year-old hanging onto a hay rack behind a runaway team of high-lifed black horses running full tilt. That's it. That is what I saw. Dick and Smoky were in a stretched out, flat belly run down a packed dirt road that would soon cross a busy highway with our tow headed Arlen hanging on for dear life. As I ran to the car I met Larry, our seven-year-old, and Grandpa Pearson, my husband's father. Larry was covered with dirt and had skinned knees. Grandpa was a blithering mess, talking both English and Swede. My husband, Milt, was on machinery on a field a mile away. Baby Linda, six weeks old, slept in her crib.

I followed the trail of dust, hands shaking, sick inside, wondering if I should have gotten Milt first. Our nearest neighbor was a mile down that road. I could see a pile of splintered boards. Wheels twisted awry lay where they had been slammed up against a fence when the horses turned in at the drive too fast. The neighbors were standing in the yard holding a trembling foam-covered team. There was no sign of an overall clad little boy. "Where is he?" I asked. Don, the neighbor, assured me there was no little boy on the rack when it turned in. I said there had to be. They said there wasn't. We turned toward the mangled pile of boards in the ditch.

Fearfully, I helped unpile those wrecked boards. There was no little boy. Then, where was he? We drove back slowly, looking in ditches and a field of corn that ran along one side. No little boy. Milt on the tractor had arrived and was trying to make

Dick & Smokey, the horses that ran away.

sense of grandpa's garbled explanation. I called for help and picked up a crying baby. Grandpa lived in Wadena after having been a farmer. He couldn't get it out of his blood and took great pleasure in coming out to help at odd jobs. Cleaning up the ditches past our place was one of them, hauling the cut hay to the cow lot.

Dick and Smoky were young, well fed, and full of soup and vinegar. They were used to Milt's voice and firm hands on the lines. Days past Grandpa Pearson had earned a reputation for having fine horses. Of late we had noticed his step not quite so firm and a bit slower. When he begged to haul the hay away Milt finally said okay. He told gramps that we absolutely did not want the boys on the rack. However, it was a nice day, everything was going well and I suppose the boys begged for a ride. Our kids and grandpa had a great relationship. No one knew that a rattly car going by too fast too close to the team would cause them to panic and take off.

Larry crawled to the edge and jumped after the first hundred feet, yelling to his brother, "Jump, Arlen!" He was still on the rack when "it went over the hill and had not been seen since." Neighbors were starting to gather in the yard, each with many ideas and taking different directions. Grandpa couldn't quit shaking, nor could I!

An hour went by with no luck. Then, along came Arlen, stumbling, dirty and bleeding he eased out of the field of head high corn. He had nothing to say other than he was awfully tired. He remembered nothing, not when he jumped or how he got into the middle of a 20 acre field of corn. A place on his forehead was puffing out the size of an orange. The doctor said it was a contusion and lanced it. I sat by his bed that night, waking him every hour as the doctor directed. We had two badly shaken little boys with a variety of bruises but, believe it or not, no broken bones.

A very contrite grandpa went home that evening, announcing "I vill neffer neffer drive anodder horse!!"

We didn't argue.

How A Bird Saved The Lost Battalion

Young Richard (Dick) Kuepers held the beautiful blue checked roller homing pigeon carefully, a gift from his father on this, his seventh birthday. The mate rested in a cage at his feet. They would take a train from Chicago to a town called "Avon", near St. Cloud, Minnesota.

Dick had grown up with a story he never tired of hearing each time it was told. Ervin Kuepers, Dick's father who had several dozen roller pigeons in a cote, told it with special feeling each time. He made Cher Ami live again. Cher Ami was a blue checked cock, English bred, who was best known of all the racer homers. The 200 men in the famous 77th Division owed their lives to him. In French Cher Ami means "Dear Friend".

It was on October 17, 1918, that the battalion advanced too far ahead of its lines into enemy territory. They were entirely surrounded, cut off from support and rations. Everything they tried failed. Soldier couriers could not penetrate the lines, flares and rockets were no help. Their condition was desperate. It was perish or surrender. Either way meant a probable death. A number of racing rollers had been sent out only to be shot down before they were out of sight, save one, Cher Ami.

The message was secured to one leg, Cher Ami was tossed up, taking many prayers for his safety with him. He arose, went straight up through a barrage of shells, circled and headed for his home loft. A bust of shrapnel spattered and Cher Ami was hit. Hearts sunk and hope faltered, then Cher Ami straightened one shattered leg and going a mile a minute flew swiftly away. Twenty-five minutes later he settled on his home loft.

Somehow, Cher Ami had managed to gain altitude beyond the range of even an enemy bullet. One leg dangled, the one with the silver canister on it had held the important message. Only 25 miles

and 25 minutes later a bloody little bird with a hole as big as a quarter in its breast landed on its back at American headquarters. He was also blinded in one eye. The 77th Division doctors spent hours patching up the brave little bird but they couldn't save his leg, so they carved a wooden one. Cher Ami's determination got him home.

Cher Ami lived 17 years. When he was fixed up it was General John J. Pershing himself who personally saw Cher Ami off for France where the French Croix de Guerre with a palm leave was bestowed on him, a one pound bird who saved a 200-man battalion. His body is on display in the Smithsonian Institute in the U.S. Museum in Washington, D.C. Dick Kuepers never tires of hearing or telling this story.

Now, two-thirds of a century later, Dick is near his pigeon cote on his place in rural Avon, sitting on an upturned box, waiting for one of his giant blue checkered rollers to come in. There is something about seeing a bird sail straight up, go into a roll, circle, then head out into that cavernous infinity called "sky" that is like nothing else for Dick. For that minute there is part of Dick that longs to go along. No, he doesn't give them names. Some owners do, but he doesn't. A man gets too close that way, and loses do happen. He calls all of his rollers just

"Bird". The story about Cher Ami came to mind, then one about Spike and Blocker.

Spike was a big grizzled grey cock hatched in France in 1918. Like Cher Ami, he served in the 77th Division. Unlike Cher Ami, he sailed through the war unscathed, carrying 52 vital messages to his home loft. His body is also mounted and in a Washington D.C. museum.

Life was different for The Blocker, a giant red cock with white markings. He was hatched in 1917, on June 15th, and lived 21 years. The Blocker was also attached to the 77th Division during the American Drive to Alsace Lorraine sector. He had an outstanding uncanny ability to somehow bring home messages through a veritable soup of artillery fire. It had something to do with his unique style. The Blocker shot straight up, high into the air, circled once, and away he went.

It was September 12, 1918, while on the Beaumont front that Blocker's fitness was needed like never before. A number of rollers had been released to carry the message only to be shot down almost as soon as they were airborne. The Blocker was the last one. German artillery was holding up American advance. On his leg The Blocker carried a message from our observation point that enabled our artillery to locate enemy guns and silence them.

This was one time the air was so alive with missiles that even The Blocker earned a purple heart. One piece carried away his right eye while another sheared off the top of his head. In pain and half blind he delivered his message and the troops were saved again. He enjoyed a long old age and his body is mounted.

It is near sundown on Dick's neat little farm. He walks over to his birds still in the cote. Shading

Richard Kuepers holding a giant homer, cock bird, dark blue check.

his eyes with his hand he looks again in the direction Bird would fly in from. Is that speck in the distance him? If it is, Bird is in trouble. There is something amiss. The cock lands with a less than graceful thud on his loft. His breast has a tear.

Although shrapnel and bullets are no longer a hazard, danger still lurks. Hawks are a menace to gentle pigeons. High, thin hard-to-see wires are strung everywhere these days. They claim many bird lives. Dick feeds Bird and sets out fresh water. He has seen tears much worse heal, so he is not concerned. Thankful his birds don't have to dodge bullets, Dick calls it a day.

CARRIER PIGEON "CHER AMI".

One of 600 birds donated by the pigeon fanciers of Great Britain for use in France during the World War. Trained by American pigeoneers and flown from American lofts, 1917-18. "Cher Ami" returned to his loft with a message dangling from the ligaments of a leg cut off by rifle or shell shot. He was also shot through the breast and died from the effects of this wound June 13, 1919.

TRANSFERRED FROM THE UNITED STATES SIGNAL CORPS.

Cheri Ami

By Harry Webb Farrington

Cher Ami, how do you do!
Listen, let me talk to you;
I'll not hurt you, don't you see?
Come a little closer to me.

Little scrawny blue and white
Messenger for men who fight,
Tell me of the deep, red scar,
There, just where no feathers are.

What about your poor left leg?
Tell me, *Cher Ami,* I beg.
Boys and girls are at a loss,
How you won that Silver Cross.

Why Won't You Die?

Nels Greenberg looked at Halvard Nyman long and hard. Why didn't the old man die? It would solve so much, especially since he had to go sometime anyhow, didn't he? As Nels saw it, Halvard was keeping soul and body together just for spite. The bone of contention was 80 acres of land near Corliss, which was mighty close to being in the middle of the state of Minnesota.

The two men had made a deal back ten years or so ago that was a life-saver for both of them. Nels was energetic, had a nice wife and six little kids but not a square inch of land or a dollar. Halvard was 74 years old, not in great health and with a don't care family who never showed up. Halvard saw the solution for both of them and proposed to Nels that if he let Halvard live with them until the end of his days. Nels would inherit the farm. Nels was overjoyed at the deal and for the first years it went along fine. Then Nels had a couple of poor crop years back to back and started borrowing money he couldn't pay back. People he owed started getting demanding and he didn't know what to do. When he asked Halvard to mortgage the land he had a fit and had been impossible to live with ever since.

Nels began to have headaches and sleep would not come. His wife, bless her, deserved better than this and so did the kids. He felt the responsibility of his family keenly. The creditors made life more miserable every day, and still Halvard wouldn't help out with a penny. Nels grew desperate to the point where he found himself planning suicide. A glance at his family and knowing it would make things worse for them made that idea intolerable. But there, just across from him, sat the old buck who had taken up room on this earth long enough. When Nels agreed to keep the old man he looked gaunt, but now with the wife's good cooking he could live forever.

Nels's mind drifted to ways to make somebody die. Shooting was messy and loud. Then he thought about some muriatic acid in the shop he'd used for welding. Halvard never turned down a swig of whiskey, which would also mask the smell and taste. Sure he was on the right track now, Nels mixed the potent, deadly mixture. Halvard tossed it down in a gulp.

Halvard went to his bed upstairs. After six hours of excruciating pain, he was dead, and Nels had a farm to support his family. He complemented himself on dispatching Halvard in way that left no tell-tale marks or scars. He looked as contrary in death as he did in life. Nels notified Nyman's son, who remarked that his dad was one cantankerous critter and thanked Nels for putting up with him all this time. Coroner Berthhold was informed, and he in turn called Dr. Haugen. After a thorough examination, they decided old Halvard had died of natural causes and left.

Life for the little family Nels loved had definitely taken a turn for the better, thanks to him. He couldn't help but strut a little. It had all happened so easily with no hitches. The hard part was having to contain all this joy to himself since he sure couldn't tell his wife. However, he did have a friend, Sam Wallace, who had once lent him twenty dollars. When no one was around, he cornered Wallace and told him. "I've got somethin' to tell you," he said, "that I wouldn't tell anybody else. You know how bad I needed money? Well, I got it settled. Just turned the calendar ahead a little bit."

When he finished he thought Wallace might say that it took some tall thinking to do a thing like that. He didn't say anything, just acted dumbfounded. After Nels went home, Sam started thinking about it. He wished Nels had not told him. Did this make

him an accomplice? He didn't know, but he knew a man in Perham who had served jury duty one time and would know. He told his friend exactly what Nels had told him. It didn't take him long to find out what to do. "Man, you gotta tell the coroner!"

Together they went to Coroner Berthhold, who called the sheriff. They all drove to Nels's newly acquired property, where they found him at home in the midst of his happy family. They called him outside to explain why they had come. Nels Greenberg denied all knowledge of such a thing and offered to go with them to Wallace's to prove it. When they faced Wallace, the sheriff told him to start talking. Nels

said, "I didn't tell you no such thing, did I Wallace? Where did they get this tangle of lies?"

"No use, Nels, might as well come clean," Wallace said. That did it. Nels sat down and told them all about it. He was up stump creek, didn't know what to do, he said.

Berthold and Haugen were truly sad. This man was desperate, not really a killer to be feared. Their duty was clear and they did it. Wallace promised Nels he would tell his wife and look in on the family now and then.

Later, Nels Greenberg was indicted for first degree murder.

That's Far Enough!

Elvin and Annie Bishop edged their way out of the Hewitt Community Hall after the Saturday night movie. A neighbor nudged Elvin, saying, "T'was something different tonight, huh? No cowboys or Indians."

"Sure was, kind of missed 'em. I don't much go for this shoot 'em up gangster stuff," Elvin replied. Elvin put a hand under Annie's elbow to help her along. She was quite heavy and her ankles gave her trouble. They had moved to Hewitt from Iowa years before, but some of that Iowan twang in their speech was still there.

Like strings of beads, car lights threaded their way out of Hewitt in four directions. The Bishop farm lay two or three miles to the north.

"Seems good to be headin' out into the quiet country after a look at that big city stuff, don't it, Ma?"

"Sure does! But you remember it was only a while back that the Hewitt bank was robbed? Crooks live everywhere. Could meet 'em right in Otis' Grocery Store in the daylight and not know 'em," Annie observed.

"Yep. They found the ones that robbed the bank in that poplar swamp west of town before they got a chance to squander a dime after goin' after all that trouble. Poor cusses," Elvin chuckled softly into the darkness at the irony of it all.

The Bishops turned into their drive. Elvin stopped up near the house like he always did. He walked toward the house to light a lamp before he helped Annie inside.

Elvin was reaching for the doorknob when he heard, "That's far enough! One more step and you're dead meat, buster! Or would you rather have your ugly head blowed off?"

Elvin froze. Ugly or not, that head had been with him for almost 81 years and he wanted to keep it. He visualized his blood oozing all over Annie's clean porch stoop, like the guy's had in the movie, and shuddered.

There were other voices. Realizing there must be more than one in there, Elvin wished he had that old deer gun on pegs over the door.

When he heard, "I been waitin' to do a number on you for a long time!" Elvin's teeth started chattering worse than when he put them in a glass. Thinking of Annie gave him a rush of adrenaline and he lunged sideways off the stoop full-length into a bed of petunias.

For a while, Elvin lay there, drowning in his own perspiration, wondering what in tarnation he had done. Or not done. He' had always helped his neighbors thresh. When Dick had to take his wife to

the doctor in the cities he had done Dick's chores for a week, not charging a dime. Over the years he had given stranded men gallons of gas, fixed at least a hundred flat tires.

Elvin dug his elbows into the dirt and pulled himself forward.

"Hold it! You kinda forgettin' I got you covered, ain't you? Wait'll we get them cee-ment overshoes on you and toss you into the East River an' see how far you get."

A fresh gush of sweat washed over Elvin. East River! Hey, these must be big time thugs from out of the county! The closest river around here was the Crow Wing, with the Long Prairie River to the south and the Buffalo River to the west. There wasn't any East River he'd ever heard of. And, even with them "cee-ment" overshoes they were talking about, he'd still be three feet above the water this time of year in any one of them.

Then Elvin made another sudden decision. To heck with it! If he was going to be gunned down anyhow, it might as well be while trying to get to the car. Getting to his feet, Elvin bent down so he was below the kitchen windowsill, then ran zig-zag to the car, the way the guy in the movie did. He landed in the car with his foot on the starter. He didn't turn on the lights.

"Sakes alive, Pa! Couldn't you find the matches or did you have to make a trip out to the biffy? Mosquitoes are awful. Say, you're headin' back to town!"

"The--the house is fulla crooks, Ma. Don't get scared, I--I'm takin' care of everything. They've been--been holdin' a gun on me! D' you tell anybody we got $50 hid in that cream can in the barn, Ma?"

"No! If I had, they'd be in the barn, not the house."

Ma was right. Elvin turned in at Del Greslin's a half-mile away. Trying not to shake too much, he told Del what was going on. Del, looking mighty puzzled, routed out his hired man. Each armed with a gun, they took the lead, lights out, and in low gear, back to Bishop's, trying to figure out who would want to hurt a good old guy like Elvin.

Carefully, Del and his man edged up to the house. After a minute, Del called out into the night, "C'mon in, Elvin. The crooks have fled and Cedric Adams is readin' the news from here, now."

After the lamp was lit and Annie helped in, Del turned off the radio, observing, "Gangbusters was extra lively tonight. You heard those crooks on a radio show!"

Still howling until they couldn't say, "Good Night," Del and his man headed back home.

Elvin went to bed but not to sleep. He had to figure out a way, somehow, to keep from showin' up in Hewitt for at least a month, by gum!

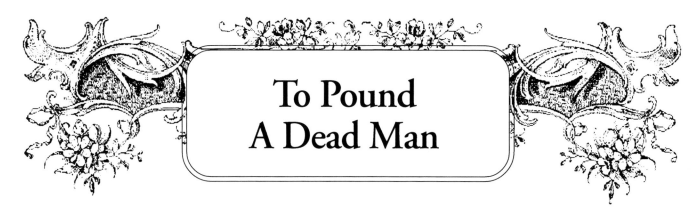

To Pound
A Dead Man

Pounding Jim Gates made Tim Lucy feel good, real good. Then a bystander called, "You're poundin' on a dead man, Tim. Jim's lights have gone out."

Tim pulled a punch to see for himself. Sure enough, old Jim was dead meat

But "I never did it!" yelled Tim, as his two brothers, Gene and Dan, came to stand beside him.

The fight started over a trifle, now there was a corpse.

It was a brisk November evening, with everybody having fun dancing at Peter Walter's house two miles out of Henning. There was a good crowd and not much room to dance, which Peter solved by giving each couple a number, then calling numbers in turn so that no more than twelve couples were on the floor at one time. When Peter called "Number 12," Jim Gates took his girl's arm, saying "That's us."

Tim Lucy was sitting there enjoying the music and just for a joke said, "Hey, not so fast. I've got number 12." Gates wheeled and came back ready to fight. When Tim saw this, he said, "Then we'll each dance half time." Gates said no way would he do that, to which Tim replied, "Then you'll just have to dance 'em all, I guess." If anybody had noticed, Tim didn't even have a girl.

It was about this time that an older brother of Gates showed up, thinking Tim was pestering his little brother. He invited Tim outside, not a good idea, given the amount of beer they had all put away, but Tim accepted. One good sock from Gates and Tim was down. Somebody pulled him off and told him to go home. The Lucy boys were halfway to their horses, when Gates hollered, "You can't bluff me!" to which Tim countered, "Well, you can't bluff me neither."

That remark set Gates off and he came tearing back, knocking Lucy down again, this time pounding his face. When Lucy managed to get on top, Jim Gates threw up his hands and fell back, dead. There was at least 20 people around and none of them thought any of Tim's punches did this. He wasn't a fighter.

Somebody said Gates had been a blamed nice guy. Wouldn't have hurt a flea. Now here he was dead at only 25, had a girl and was paying on a farm and everything.

Tim Lucy had a nice wife and six kids. He was 45 and far more apt to break up a fight than start one. He wasn't a killer. Everybody said so.

When Coroner Bedford got a look at Gates it didn't clear up the story, because he said Gates had been hit with something that made deep holes just behind each ear, and he more than likely died instantly.

The coroner's jury, consisting of six men concluded Gates had been struck with a blunt instrument, like a sling shot. Several witnesses said they saw Gene do it. Finally, on November 2, 1887, on a Wednesday morning, Dan and Gene were arraigned in Judge Shout's court. Tim Lucy was charged an accessory to the crime.

How Gates could have been hit hard twice, when no weapon was found, and no one seeing one, has never been cleared up.

Ground His Father To Bits

Sigverd Pearson was nine years old that fateful day he ground his own father to bits. Being a terrible accident did nothing to make it easier to bear. Wherever he went people pointed him out, saying "That's him! Put his own pa through the grinder, he did." As soon as Sigverd was old enough, while still a teenager, he left Sweden for the United States, where he would be free of that horrible label. When I was eighteen he became my father-in-law. Dad Pearson was a treasure trove of stories, all true.

The story Dad tried for 92 years to forget happened when he was nine years old. During those days farmers ground grain in a big hopper, many bushels at a time since they had to take turns with the mill. A belt ran from the hopper inside the barn to a wheel pulled round and round by a horse who in this way provided power. The young lad in the family kept the horse moving, a tiresome job for both boy and horse.

It was an unseasonably hot day and both boy and horse were lazy, wanting a drink. Shouts from inside the barn brought Sigverd wide awake. He urged the horse to go faster. More screams and shouting and a neighbor yanked the horse to a halt. Sigverd stepped into the barn to a sight he could never bring himself to fully describe. His father was in the grinder head first. He saw a mangled piece of shirt, a bloody hand. The straw must have gotten bunched up and pa was trying to free it when the sharp knives caught his sleeve. Dad jumped that part of the story by saying "It--It was awful!" We didn't press him for more details. At that point he usually found something to do elsewhere.

A more cheerful one of Dad's stories was about a preacher who claimed to be on a first name basis with God, who supposedly provided him with fire and brimstone sermons to be preached. On one Sunday preacher came with important news to impart that got the undivided attention of the most lax. God himself, he claimed, was going to come on a particular date to sweep up in one swoop all of the

Sigverd Pearson

true believers that he found there. The site was a small hill not far from the Pearson farm. Only a small fee that covered the whole family was mentioned.

Such news spread like wild fire. That was before the terrible accident so the entire Pearson family of three girls and two boys with their parents flew around getting things ready for Judgment Day. Not a harsh word was spoken. The women in the family reclaimed the husky brown loaves of bread they had baked for the winter in the big brick oven that filled one end of a room. The men knocked down rails from pens of pigs, cows, and horses, making feed available to them. The preacher hadn't said what provisions had been made for the critters. When Margit wanted to take her pet cat along, they said "Better not."

Not long after sun up on that proper day neighbors for miles came, dressed in their Sunday

best. Not a single mother warned about tearing Sunday cloths, or getting dirty. Halaleuyah! It didn't matter anymore. Men agreed this was a fine time to stop the world from making another round on its axis. There wasn't going to be much of a grain crop, anyhow. Now, who cared? As the sun climbed toward it's zenith it got warmer. Dad remembers falling asleep on the soft grass. The big folks were trying to recall if "Preacher" had mentioned a time for the pick-up? And, where was he? Many of the women had joined the kids on the soft grass, men were scuffling restlessly around, more than one kid was bawling. From the vantage of the hill top they could see their animals, all mixed up, the Pearson's with the Olson's, Olson's with Petersons, Ostlunds with all the rest. It was a mess.

The sun was starting to sink when they started home. Quietly, no longer a wonderful happening. They didn't look at one another, wondering how much each family had paid for this debacle. At this juncture in his story Dad always laughed. He could still remember trying to chase their livestock back where it belonged without the Olson, Peterson, or Ostlunds' stuff. Mother and the girls had it hardest. Their winter's provisions were gone, eaten up by the hogs. The flour barrel was empty. The chickens were all roosting so high up in the trees they didn't even have an egg to fry.

Dad's spell of telling stories ended about here. He'd say, "Yeah, that was quite a day. Ma was worn out and pa--well, pa wasn't there more than a week after that."

Philosophy of Life

by

Grace Hartley

God in His goodness hath taught me to see
The goodness in others and then,
He asks me to give, to do and to live
For the welfare of my fellow men.

God in His power hath given me strength,
Given me courage to dare
To walk down life's road and shoulder the load
Of someone who's strength faltered here.

Written Grace Hartley, poet laureate of the University of South Dakota,
while a resident of Shady Lane Nursing Home in the early 80's.

Fergus Falls, A Nice Little Village

We bought a little place and 100 sheep. Since there was only one building on the place and it was early winter, we moved into the south end, the sheep in the other. We got along fine, although their baa-baa's nearly drove us crazy. We learned to block it out.

My name is "Martha Hadley". Pa and ma are Mr. and Mrs. Hiram Hadley. They lived in a log house on another man's land. That's where I was born in 1844. I started school when I was five and only had to walk a mile. Later I went to a school in Cray Mills and when I was 18 taught a few years. I learned to sew, which I could do at home because ma was getting worse. A big tumor caused her to be sick a long time, until she died on October 15, 1857.

I married Orly Gouldin at Hopkinton on the fourth of July, 1868. Until we could buy a place we lived with his brother for a spell and then to his parents' place in Southville until spring. I was deliriously happy when Orly bought a little place three miles south of Hopkinton. There was no house so we moved into an old house so decrepit I wondered that it still stood. You can bet Orly went right to work choppin' logs for our new house. On July 14, 1871, our oldest child was born in the old house.

About six weeks after the new house was built, Anna Olivia was born and a month later we was aboard a wagon train headed toward all that good land in Minnesota to find us a place to settle on. That sure sounded good. Each family gave the scout $5.00. We had to go special that day when we met 70 men and women also in the train. We had never seen any of them before. Parting with people we had come over on the boat with was hard. I was not very strong and my baby was only two months old. Orly bought a ticket for me and the baby so we could ride passenger class. He and Winson went steerage. They stayed in the box car with their cattle. It was mostly a pleasant trip except at night.

On that night the sea's were high and rough. There were 12 horses aboard that panicked when a board plank fell down among them. They kicked and jumped a long time. A spooked horse is dangerous, I can tell you! Orly was sick but they came up after him to help. The children and I stayed in bed laying flat. I heard I wouldn't get sick that way and I didn't. We changed boats in Cleveland so we stayed in a hotel, feeling like rich folks. We were on that boat 10 days. I made friends with Mr. and Mrs. Brown who had children a bit older than ours. The little ones under two got to ride free which helped. Watching the little ones from falling overboard was a full time job. They wanted to see the water.

The night we stayed in Cleveland a fire bell rang. I had never seen a real fire truck. Orly and I dressed, locked the children in the room, and went to see the fire. The next day it was back on the boat for us. It took three days to load over. Our trip took us through all of the lakes but Michigan. It took forever getting through the canal. We could go on shore, look around, and get back again. We watched Indians fish with little scoop nets. We were tired but excited. Our next stop in Duluth there would be a man who had chosen our farm for us. I could hardly wait. Orly pretended not to be excited but he couldn't fool me... Forty families stayed in the immigrant house in Duluth.

The house was big and empty, with bunks nailed to the wall all around. The men found an old stove and brought it in so we could cook. After three days Mr Sherwin, our pilot came. The train was made up of a baggage car and one car for our 12 horses, and the caboose for people. We spread blankets on the floor. It was night and a few miles out was a new

road. A sink hole lay in wait and our baggage car went into it. We were glad it wasn't the one with the horses. Another train backed up to the hole on the other side of the track. A frail temporary track had been laid around the hole and a hand car moved our stuff from one car to the other. It took all day. We women had to try somehow to make a supper and breakfast for these, hard working men....and nothing to work with!

We arrived in Furgus Falls [Fergus Falls] which looked like a nice little village with mostly log houses. We stopped in a grove where people were having a picnic. The men went on so each could choose his homestead. Because Orly had been a soldier he got 160 acres instead of 80 like the others. While in Fergus Falls Orly traded our horse and wagon for a yoke of oxen and a covered wagon.

We left the morning of the 20th of July. Our covered box served as our bedroom. Orly cut grass and I filled a tick I made, we put it in the wagon box then I put a feather bed on top of it. The next day he went to work building a shanty. He got poles from a grove three miles away. The next day he went to work where he left off the night before putting up crotchets into the ground with poles on top. He cut grass 3' high, made it into bundles, and stood them around for the top and sides.

Our furniture came, next. I was so proud of him. Our wood packing boxes were turned into a cross legged table and stools, and a cupboard. He made a fireplace with a hook to hang the pan with hot ashes and coals on top. I could not make pie this way but everyone bragged about my bread. Halfway through the morning a storm came up. I never saw worse wind, lightening and thunder. It took the sides off the house and twisted the hoops that went over the wagon. I was afraid our roof was coming down so Orly took the straw tick and put it away from the house. The baby and I sat on it, and he carried blankets from the house to throw over us. After it was over he took us to the Robben's place a mile away. He had a board shanty, but we found it leaked, too. At least he had a stove to get warm on.

Two weeks later I became terribly sick in my wagon box bed. A doctor was 10 miles away. Our shanty was so wrecked the neighbors helped Orly set up a real bed and stove out in the yard. Mrs. Bates took my baby and Mrs. Brown took Frank, who was three. The doctor's calls costing $18. I was not getting better. Orly told the doctor that he need not come back. Orly said that he was going to talk to the Lord an' do what He directed. Orly said he felt directed to take a few handfuls of bark off the green white oak logs in the yard. He steamed this and put in spice and a lump of sugar. I was given a teaspoon of this every hour. It cured me. Orly had to take a tub of laundry down to the lake to wash it. He hired a girl that I could not talk to. We had to go a mile for milk. Mrs. Brown brought my baby back. She came crying because she thought I was not getting better. Not only did I get better, but I could nurse my baby again!

Mr. Sherman helped Orly build a 12' x 16' half roof house over us. We had to face it that we had nothing to live on until the next harvest. We hadn't got there in time to plant anything. We met a family halfway between us and Fergus Falls who lived there before the Indian massacre. They claimed anybody who couldn't eat muskrat should starve. Orly set out a dozen traps. He intended to make trapping a winter job. We cooked the first one he caught. Mr. Sherman stayed and Frank thought it delicious. The rest of us could hardly swallow it.

In June my father and Uncle Aaron Shaw went to Minneapolis. Uncle had three children there. On the same train with them was a 40 pound box of maple sugar. It was early May. I was glad to see father and really needed the sugar. Praise God, we had wonderful crops that year. We sorely needed a house and barn. We had a sod stable like the house and stacked hay outside. I forgot that on the brightest day storm clouds gather. That fall Dr. Goodale started holding special meetings. The Presbytery said they would help us build a church. Our little community needed one. One woman who said she was a Christian said a school should come first. Orly thought she

was making fun of him. During this time a Catholic woman a half-mile from us kept asking Orly for help. He went often.

The evening of January, 1874, the minister came up and had a service. Orly took the team and we went, taking our neighbor and his wife. Orly talked a little, and when the meeting closed asked Dr. Goodale to go home with us. He said he had promised another family but would come next time. Then Orly went to my cousin, Horace Shaw and wife, and asked them to go home with us but they could not. Mr. Vanorman stopped to help take care of the team. I put the children to bed and we all retired. About midnight our dog who slept in the house began to bark, which was unusual. Orly got up to see what was the reason. He went outside and I could hear him talking to somebody.

When I asked Orly who he had been talking to, he said "It was the Lord. He has told me what I should do." He rambled on then got quiet. I knew his mind had left him and was afraid. He had been working very hard in the cold, maybe it was that, I thought. There was an odd light in his eyes I had never seen there before. Maybe he would be straight in the morning after a good sleep. I slept very little that night.

All was quiet until 7 o' clock. Then Orly started in again. He said we were going to have a three day storm. It was snowing hard. He said a lot of people were coming but he was going back to bed. He said "Don't go to the barn, let the cattle all die. They are likely all dead now." He ordered me to go to the door and call that old hypocrite. Then he asked me to get the bible and read to him. He got real agitated. I didn't know what to do. I had never seen anyone like this before. I wished Dr. Goodale had come home with us. The kids knew something was wrong and started to cry. Getting up, Orly used his boot to bash in the top of the stove. Pieces fell on the floor. A chair took his attention. He slammed it on the wall and broke it. Next, he grabbed an overhead beam and began to swing on it. He jammed his hand onto a pan hanging on the wall, cutting his fingers

deep. I held his arm and started to cry when he headed toward the children.

It was snowing like crazy outside. What could I do?

Then Orly pulled Henry, 11 months, out of bed. He threw him on the floor with the broken parts of the stove. I screamed. He acted as if I wasn't there. He yanked Anna and Frank up and threw them down with Henry. I begged him to stop. I said "Don't kill them!! They haven't done anything. PLEASE, Orly!"

He only turned, looked at me with those strange eyes, saying "I know, but I have to kill all of you. He told me to last night." He grabbed me by the arm and pulled me toward the door. He tried to set our dog on me. I was a little afraid of the dog, but I told him to lay down and he did. Then, Orly said "I see you've got the dog under your control and against me."

Frank and Anne climbed back into their bed, crying. Orly picked up Henry and put him in bed, saying, "You see? He is not hurt. I have some special miracle working in me. I must go again and talk to the Lord, but I'll be back." Without stopping for warm clothes he walked out into the blizzard in his night clothes. I knew, he'd soon be back.

I waited a bit and went to the door. I couldn't see him. I knew he wouldn't get far in this storm. I felt sick and sat on the edge of a bunk. Our only chair was broken.. I decided Orly must have made it to the barn. I dressed the children in all of their clothes, and put them back to bed. I fed them as much bread and milk as they could eat before it froze and put a loaf of bread in bed with them. There was no fire and it was cold, cold. We all were exhausted. I knew what I had to do. Henry looked blue and my milk had dried up with no food and so much stress. I could not stand the cold long enough to thaw milk over the lamp. I was surprised how peacefully the children stayed in bed. I got up often to look at the storm.

It slacked off and by midnight a bit of moon was showing. As soon as it was a little light I made the children promise not to leave the bed, took Henry

bundled up, and started out. I went straight across the lake to Vanornam's. It was Sunday and they were still in bed. Snow was brushed up against the door so I knew they were there. They let me right in. They were really shocked to hear the news because they had gone to church with us on Friday night. They poked the fire and I was soon warm. Mr. Vanorman went right over to get Frank and Anne. He went past Mr. Robbin's and Mr. Smith's, who went over to feed the cattle.

Then they started looking for Orly. They found him beside the road, just a few yards from home. The children and I went to Mr. Robbins and they took Orly to Mrs. Vanornam's to prepare him for burial. Then they went into Fergus Falls to tell people and talk to the preacher. The preacher came right out to see me. He said he wished that he had

come home for the night when Orly asked him. He assured me that the Lord had been with us that night.

The month of October came and I married Milton Snell. His first wife was Elnore Goulding, a half-sister to Orly. We lived together for 15 years. He had four children and with my three we had quite a family. In March I got a letter from my brother, Franklin, that I had to go back and prove I owned my place because he had heard someone talking of jumping my claim. In April I went back to the land office. I took Orly's discharge paper along. That made the five years needed to get a deed. I rented it to Mr. Robbins for two years for $100.

One by one our children grew up and left our nest. Milton was a good father and husband. We sold the farm and went to live in Fergus Falls, a nice little village.

Tommy Dunn's Last Message

"A strong torrid wind caused our houses on the north west end of town to burst into flame; the very air was on fire. The wind blew water from our hoses. Be on guard! The fire is here; scarcely a mile away; and the wind is picking up. Our town is doomed!" A few minutes later Tommy Dunn sent the message to Branum, "I'm afraid I stayed too long." Following the message, he ran for his life. He had only gone six blocks when, according to reports, a great fireball carried by a stiff wind seemed to fall from the sky on the depot. Tommy was charred.

The blast was so hot coins left in pockets were melted, which requires a temperature of 1,500 degrees Fahrenheit. Nails were melted. Some people made it to safety by clinging to the outsides of St. Paul-Duluth and Eastern Minnesota trains. A gravel pit that held three feet of water saved at least 100.

Between 4:00 and 4:27 a train headed from Hinckley to Superior, a precarious trip. On the first 14 miles of railroad no less than 19 wooden bridges had to be crossed. A train brakeman examined each bridge for safety before the train crossed. The Kettle River Bridge was already on fire. The brakeman made a speedy evaluation and told the engineer "You've got about five minutes before she goes. Good luck!" The northeast end of the bridge fell seconds after the train passed.

The train saved 478 people on a seven-hour 70-mile trip to West Superior, thanks to Tommy Dunn, who saved no room for himself.

Tucker's Fire

The disastrous fire everyone feared happened in June, 1910. Each year, the town of Clara City had increased its efforts to enforce fire protection. Some didn't cooperate.

The fire began in Stager's Meat Market, which was still owned by a Mr. Tucker. Someone spilled some gasoline, causing an explosion that burned the Tucker building to the ground as well as damaging two saloons and the Meyer Building.

Jack Stager's mother was at the pump filling pails, tubs, wash boilers and anything else that would hold a little water to be carried up the stairs or a ladder to throw on the fire. Jack's father had severe burns. A brigade of young boys carried items from McCorks store across the street from the depot.

Jack and Sander Luures were on ladders when Sander fell from the ladder. By grabbing Sander's legs, Jack saved him from falling 30 feet.

Tucker's Fire

Tucker's Store

Enkema Building

Treed By A Grizzly

Juan hated himself. In a place crowded with trees, why did he pick the spindliest, most anemic one of the bunch to climb? Because it was the closest, he answered himself, and he could almost feel the breath of that grizzly. Pulling himself up in the tree did not help much. The bear's claws were only inches from the toe of his shoe. He had not been hunting grizzles. Neither had the man who lay dead by the canyon wall. Juan was not Apache but considered himself one because he had been taught by them.

After he was set free by the Proclamation Emancipation, he became a professional hunter. He had a Spanish musket. Most Indians were not allowed to carry one. During the Civil War, times were good in New Mexico. After the war, two or three wagon trains a day came down the trail. Game became scarce and the wagoners arrogant. Juan joined the Apaches and Utes to rob wagon trains only after hearing how white men were raping Indian women.

Juan and Chagon, the dead man in the canyon, spent the winter fairly comfortable in their hogan of logs and mud. Juan had two hundred rounds of caps and balls for his smoothbore musket, and Chagon had a good bow and arrow. They never wanted for meat. It was a good life, although they would have liked better food and the companionship of their women. They had already killed two sheep that winter and now, on this spring morning, they hankered for elk. A short distance from their hogan they found trails of a bull elk. It was a big bull but thin and gaunt. Its antlers were chalky, almost ready to shed.

When the elk turned broadside, Juan fired. The bull jumped violently, then galloped up the canyon. Suddenly he collapsed and died. Juan and Chagon butchered him on the spot. They tied the pieces they wanted high up in a cottonwood, then continued their hunt for a sheep. The big horns had moved. The hunters went back to the hogan empty handed. Out of the shadows of the canyon wall came low growl, then a big bear was upon them. Chagon reached for an arrow behind his back but the bear attacked him and he died without a sound.

While the grizzly was reaching down to bite his friend, Juan ran back a few steps, cocked his musket and fired straight at the grizzly. The smoke cleared, the bear saw Juan and charged. Dropping the gun Juan made for the nearest tree. He wished it were bigger, or he had been able to get to the next tree. Juan climbed for all he was worth until he reached a puny fork that had to do. The grizzly raised up on his hind legs, reaching for Juan's feet. A curved claw hooked one of his moccasins and ripped the shoe away. Juan felt a stinging pain. He could see hair matted with blood on the bear's hump where his shot had landed. In a few bites the bear ripped away almost half of the trunk of the tree right below the crotch where Juan clung. He could feel the tree shiver. A few more like that and the tree would be down.

Juan steadied himself between two spreading limbs above the crotch, well within the reach of those claws. When the tree swayed a bundle of meat came thundering down. Holding on with one hand Juan drew his hunting knives and cut a strip from the bundle. Then he carefully dropped it on the bear's head. The bear jumped back, landing on all fours. With a ferocious growl he pummeled the meat, shaking it from side to side. Finally, the big beast lay full length on his belly as he gulped down huge chunks.

Tree trunks on which the elk meat was tied showed deep claw marks. "When the brute has his fill he will go away," Juan told himself. The bear did not leave. Not even after the last scrap was gone. As dark fell the bear savagely attacked the body of Chagon, biting deep holes into the body, then turning it over. He did not eat the body but lay down beside

it as if to guard his catch. Juan removed his head band to tie around his injured foot. He pulled the collar up around his neck against a cold wind.

Juan promised himself that by morning the grizzly would be gone and then he could retrieve his gun and bury the body of his friend in one of the cracks along the canyon wall as the Apaches did. At last dawn came. The grizzly still crouched beneath the overhead. Juan was so cramped and stiff he had to move just a little. Cautiously, he slowly put one foot, then the other into the crotch of the tree to straighten his legs. At the least movement the grizzly came lumbering out of the shadows with lightening speed. He reared on hind legs and clawed at the tree, trying to reach the man. Juan jerked his feet up an instant before the claws hit that spot. Again, the bear started gnawing the tree. A few more bites and the tree would fall. Juan prayed in a low voice to the Christian God of the Gonzales family who raised him and did not neglect the Apache god of the mountains. He needed all of the help he could get!

Then, miracles of miracles, the grizzly stopped biting and stood motionless against the tree, his black muzzle wrinkling back and forth. He was smelling something. At last he dropped back to all fours and went to another tree, the one where another bundle of meat hung. All that day the bear worried the trunk of that tree. Twice he walked to the body of Chagon to bite into it, but he always came back. When night fell the second day it found the grizzly still guarding its prize. Juan felt weak. He needed water. He was desperate for sleep. His endurance was

about to end, then he would see that stiff body and cling all the tighter to his tree. A stiff cold wind came down the canyon. The tree was swaying...would it break?

A couple of hours later the grizzly came to the foot of the tree and looked up. His eyes were blood shot. Juan thought, he has come to finish me off. In a little while I will look like Chagon. Without preamble, the grizzly looked up, wrinkled his nose one more time then bounded down the canyon. Bears are clever, was it a trick? Taking a chance, Juan fell to the ground. His legs were numb and would not hold him up. He crawled to where his musket lay. He reloaded the musket and put a cap on the nipple. A day later Juan returned to bury his friend.

From now on there would be no refuge in this canyon for Apaches. No Indian would ever hunt there again. The big grizzly was evil medicine.

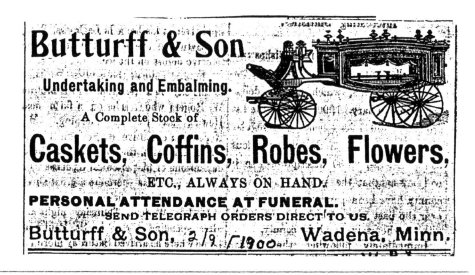

A Moo Moo Here: A Moo Moo There

On a foggy Tuesday morning in Osakis, Minnesota, in 1903, 600 Montana Longhorns were everywhere, doing everything but jumping over the moon. It was 6:00 a.m. The train, with most of the crew still asleep, had stopped to take on water. A hobo had been hired for extra help. Not being able to sleep, because of a painful boil, the hobo was awake when the powerful headlights of the stock extra Number 523 came thundering toward them on the same tracks. He roused the crew, who jumped to safety just in time.

The caboose and the next two cars were smashed and over turned. The engineer and brakeman of 523 jumped just in time. Why the fireman didn't follow suite is a mystery. He stayed aboard while the engine twisted its way down a 10 foot embankment. Other cars jackknifed. The fireman had both legs broken and a severe head wound.

To make the crash especially unique, 600 angry head of longhorns thrashed their way through streets, into yards and over fences, bellowing their resentment at being dumped out like this. A couple of dozen were strung along the tracks. Thirty of them were sufficiently hurt to be destroyed. The public was terrified! Schools closed early, matrons locked themselves in their houses, drunks in the saloons swore they had had one drink too many, seeing all those mad bulls in quiet little Osakis.

Despite the confusion, the town pulled itself together and tried to act normal by the end of the day. Every available man herded cattle toward a stockyard that was much too small. Dead cattle were pushed into a hole on the Jake Bowman farm. The train wrecking crew came at noon the next day. The injured fireman, Peter Netzing, had to be pried out of the wreckage and rushed to Osakis Woodward Hospital.

Pete doesn't begrudge all that happened one bit, because he saw Mrs. Woodward's daughter and forgot his ailments pronto. A few months later, after he was up again, he made her his wife.

This was the scene of the 1903 train wreck at Osakis.

Railroad Man

On January 7, 1907, a young man watched a mighty steam locomotive chug its way north out of the roundhouse at Staples, Minnesota. Sixty-two years, four months, and twenty-three days later he glided into the same yards, from the same direction, behind the smooth pull of a powerful diesel, finishing his last run. "Goin' down those metal steps for the last time wasn't easy," Charlie recalls.

Charles C. Shinkle was born on July 23, 1879, in Renville County, Minnesota. His first wife died, leaving him with a son. On August 23, 1928, Charles married Louise Voltz of Staples and to them two daughters were born.

After working several months in the yards Charlie's persistence paid off. He was hired on as a fireman. He says it gave him at least a faint idea of what hell must be like. In June 1921, Charlie stepped up to engineer, a position he held until twelve years before his retirement, at which time he was made Chief Head Engineer of trains One and Two. Charlie, with the exception of a 14-month stretch in the army spent in the Philippines (no Philodendrons in <u>his</u> house ever, you bet!), he was employed exclusively by the Northern Pacific Railroad. Although his career began and ended in Staples, he changed locale many times over the intervening years.

Spokane and Seattle, on the Pasco Division, meant his trains battled a mountain run that sometimes called for four mammoth engines, a couple pulling and a couple pushing. If the tracks were icy and they ran out of sand in these mountains, it was every engineer's nightmare, and was one story that was every bit as bad as the way it was described.

Charlie "measured the plains" from Williston and Mandan, and coped with more snow on the Duluth run than he still enjoys thinking about. He worked out of St. Paul to Fargo in the early days un-

til he "ran out of tracks."

Serious Accidents? Which one d'you want to hear about first? Besides, when a train is one of the components there ain't no other kind. Charlie always made good use of the whistle, to let everything that could move know he was coming. Yet, you'd be surprised at the stuff that would just stand there and get splattered! Cows, horses, even a buffalo or two, years ago. The worst--the *very* worst--was seeing a car on the tracks, knowing that you couldn't stop! Loaded, it took four or five miles on flat land to stop. That's when he prayed like crazy that it was an abandoned car! His prayers weren't always answered.

A real serious accident happened February

Charlie Shinkle

Charlie Shinkle

4, 1927, at Edgeley, North Dakota, while Charlie was running snowplow.

A wall of snow lay ahead in a huge bank. The only way to get through it was to take a run for it, which was the way big banks were usually broken open. This one was so hardened by days of a stiff wind that the impact flipped the locomotive end for end, splitting it wide open. His fireman was killed. Charlie got bumps, cuts, and scratches when the cab flew over his head.

Let's talk about something else!

Well, did anything funny happen? Charlie starts to grin.

"Yeah, heh, heh, heh. There was this one boss, kind of an inspector, see? Couple of times a year he would ride along to check everybody and every operation out. That's back when we slept and ate right on the train around the clock. This guy was up for a promotion and was out to brown-nose the big shots in the company. He went over the cook's grocery lists two or three times, weeding out everything but the same old common foods that we were tired of eating. Made the cook mad, too. The guys hated his tracks.

"Somewhere up around Minot it snowed and blowed for three days and we got drifted in. After the second day of regular meals the cook started cuttin' down. Then he got an idea! He gave us guys the wink and started cookn' thin. Real thin! He sneaked us sandwiches after we went to bed.

"After the first three days the guys started to yell, but each day the fare was worse until all the cook served was coffee so thin you could read 'The Railroad Times' through it and sloppy oatmeal. Out was out, see? He couldn't cook what had been cut from his list, cook explained. The guy hated oatmeal. Said his bowels was like cement and he'd have to head for the nearest hospital as soon as we got out. I tell'ya, the crew was in stitches. They got us out after six days. That was the last grocery order ever cut."

As Charlie sees it, engineering is still the best occupation a man can have, though most of the responsibility, and thus the challenge, has gone out of it. Why? A man doesn't have to think anymore, that's why. At the first hint of trouble all the engineer does is grab the phone at his elbow and yell, "What'll I do?" to a boss who turns to a computer supposed to stop other trains on the track, sidetrack 'em, or what-

ever.

Years ago an engineer had to get himself out of trouble by using his head. Another thing: These fellows can see where they're goin'! So much of the time, with the old locomotives, visibility was almost nil because of the coal smoke that blowed back over the engine. The diesel engine is one of the most important inventions of the century.

During the years it wasn't all work. Charlie and Louise, with their family, fished and camped out every chance they got. They were members of The Faith Lutheran Church of Staples. Louise headed the Lady Engineers and was a charter member of the Eastern Star, Chapter Four. Charlie was a Life Brotherhood Member of Eastern Star, secretary-treasurer of the Brotherhood for nine years, and on the executive and legislative boards so long he can't remember when he started. Add to this, the Masons, the Shriners, and the Scottish Rite.

The day a policeman came to their door to inform them that their daughter Elaine had died, Louise crumpled, never to speak, walk, or take care of herself again. Her stroke blots out for Charlie any other bad thing that ever happened to him.

Retired now, Charlie sold their home and with Louise entered a nursing home. There, he saw that she had everything to make her comfortable, sitting with her several hours each day. In the lounge, he smoked big black cigars while he read the news. He lambasted those "rabble-rousers" who persisted in marching across his TV screen each newscast.

Before he died, well past ninety, Charles C. Shinkle was presented with a sixty-year pin set with diamonds by Charles Gilespie and Jim Schroeder of Staples on behalf of the Brotherhood of Locomotive Engineers and Firemen.

Whenever anyone asked to see his pin, after a couple of swipes acrossed his sleeve to shine her up a bit, Charlie would hand it over, saying "There she is!"

The time-honored test of ascertaining whether a "right" choice has been made is, in retrospect, would one follow the same path in the same way, again?

Charlie's stock reply was always an emphatic, "Do it again! D'you mean there is *another* satisfyin' way of makin' a livin'?"

Withered Roses

Of all the 2,000 withered roses, in the 250 and 300 brothels in Chicago in 1867, Lou Harper had to be among the most wilted. Along with being a bit shop worn, Lou ran the city's first parlor house. It was full of expensive trappings. She called it the "Mansion." If Madame Harper's establishment was the fanciest, it was also the highest priced. Her girls wore long ball gowns of silk and satins. She catered to business and professional men, to the rich young man-about-town who seeks illicit pleasures.

Brothels in Chicago during the 1860's were at an all time high. It was believed that officers failed to arrest more than half of the prostitutes in a year. The low dens were found on Monroe, Wells, Clarke, Dearborn, and Quincy, and many more stalls were populated with street walkers. They maintained living and business quarters on the top floors of stores and business buildings and walked the streets at any hour of the night or day. They boldly asked every man they met and yelled insults to those who ignored them. Confidence men, sneak thieves, harpies, pick pockets and shoplifters thrived in this element.

None of the other brothels equaled Lou Harper's Mansion, but there were several who frequented the same class and were almost as popular. There was Kate Anderson's Senate, the houses run by Mollie Trussell and Rose Lovejoy's place on Fourth Avenue. A big blowsey known as "Mountain Nel", sang love songs and was Rose Lovejoy's bouncer. Madam Stewart opened her house in 1862, then after a dozen prosperous years her career came to a screeching halt, on July 11, 1868. On the afternoon of that day Constable Monroe Donahue and G.O. Dresser, a justice of the peace, visited the house and while the justice was talking to one of the girls Donahue and Madame Stewart played euchre and had drinks. After several games, with as many bottles of wine emptied, the Madame accused the constable of cheating, after which he tried to choke her. She snatched a revolver from under her pillow and shot him dead as a door nail right in the heart.

The Madame was arrested, but on July 15, was brought to Circuit Court on a writ of habeas corpus. She was set free after a policeman testified as

MARY HASTINGS AND ONE OF HER BROTHELS

to finger marks on her throat. The judge ruled that she had not "forfeited her rights by resorting to the disreputable life of a cyprian."

The largest bordello in Chicago before the great fire was the notorious Ramrod Hall, a rambling wooden building. It was kept by Kate Hawkins, who ruled her flock with a horse whip. She seldom had fewer than 30 girls and sometimes as high as 50, all of whom lived in the house. It was not unusual for a man to be slugged and robbed. Booze flowed and everyone was usually drunk. Police were called at least once every evening.

The biggest fight at Ramrod happened on March 21, 1871. The *Times* described Mary Woodridge as a "very lucrative piece of furniture," and said she was leaving Ramrod to be married. Madame Hawkins whipped the girl and locked her in her room. The girl's friends came to help and a free-for-all fight broke loose. Harlots, pimps, and even customers were using fists, feet, beer bottles, and furniture to fight with. The police arrived to find Ramrod Hall wrecked and half of the crowd either drunk or unconscious on the floor.

Madame Jennie Standish's place on Welle Street and Belle Jones' den boasted of employing "the oldest drones in the world." They were said to be past 60. Shilowe Alley, the Chicago Patch, and Mother Connally's Patch were destroyed by the big fire. Within a decade they were not only all back...but there were more of them! The new batch were given such names as Black Hole, Little Cheyenne, The Bad Lands, Satan's Mile, Bill's Avenue, and Dead Man's Alley.

The two upper rooms of the "Marble Front" on Monroe Street was the abode of Waterface Jack, also known as the "Millionaire Streetwalker," who boasted walking streets every night, rain or shine, for ten years. The *Chicago Street Gazette*, in 1877, wrote that Waterface Jack had $22,000 in the bank, every cent of which she had picked up (so to speak) on the streets of Chicago, adding that it was said to her credit that she never stole a cent and never got drunk in her life. She was described as a pug nosed, ugly-looking little critter, but for all that she prospered in her

INTERIOR OF A PANEL-HOUSE

wretched business, and stood before the world the richest street walker in existence.

Of all the brothels in Chicago's old red light district, the ones that gave police the most trouble were the panel-houses. These were robbing dens, made for that purpose. They had sliding panels in doors and interior walls. A thief could disappear in a flash. These rooms had no furniture other than a bed and a chair, with the chair placed near a sliding panel where the customer left his clothes. It was claimed that as much as $1,500,000 was stolen each year.

It was Detective Clifton Woodridge who is given credit for doing away with panel houses. He was sometimes very funny, like the time he arrested a girl on the street, then climbed on the shoulders of a

thief he had captured and rode to jail. He had 75 disguises he kept in the squad room. He carried two guns and although he never killed anybody; he put bullets in many arms, legs, and behinds.

During the early 1890's, Detective Woolridge broke up one of the most extraordinary gangs of criminals that ever settled in Chicago. A half-dozen black women, called "foot pads," prowled everywhere,

even the south side, before they were sent to jail. They worked in pairs and were armed with revolvers, razors, brass knuckles, knives, and sawed-off baseball bats. Their favorite trick was to slash a victims knuckles with a razor if he didn't raise his arm fast enough.

It appeared that those roses who withered were also plenty stupid!

Killer Komula

Taking her husband, Andrew , lunch and a cool drink on that hot afternoon of July 21, 1936, proved to be fatal for Esther Komula. He killed her.

The murder took place in Red Eye Township on the Komula farm north and east of Sebeka, Minnesota. By his own admission, Komula climbed down from his tractor, the better to smash Esther's head to a pulp with the fruit jar she carried the cool drink in. Cut and bleeding, she begged for her life, for the sake of their children.

At this point, according to Komula, they made up, or at least so Esther thought. He kissed her, didn't he? Then he walked 40 feet to a mower, took a hammer out of the tool box, and walked back. Like a savage he beat her head in, dragged her to a clump of trees, and took off.

In the house, the five Komula children, were petrified with fear. Their parents quarreled, but their father had never before told them they would never see their mother again. The two oldest girls made their way to the field. The tractor sat there. Their father was gone and so was their mother. They saw a trail of blood and followed to where their mother lay in a pool of blood, moving slightly. Tearing strips from her dress, they tried to stop the blood. It was no use. That's when they ran to a neighbor for help.

Esther Komula was taken to Welsey Hospi-

tal in Wadena where for two weeks she put up a valiant fight for her life. Although her skull had been fractured and she had gone through an operation that took ten square inches of bone, she was able to talk to doctors. She had long been afraid of her husband.

On the day he had thrown what he believed to be his dead wife's body in the trees, Andrew took off in his car. For the next nine months, he rambled here and there, always afraid of being caught. He first spent some time in Winona working on a farm, then moved to Ada, which he left when a plane flew over too low, moving from Minnesota to LaCrosse, Wisconsin. During this time, an all points bulletin was out on him and they were looking for him as far as Oregon and Alaska.

The tension, along with the wish to see his children, became so strong that he risked a train ride to Verndale, then hitched a ride to his brother's farm in Red Eye Township. He spent Sunday night there. Convinced he would never get away, Komula walked into Sheriff John Bergston's office in Wadena, the county seat on April 29, 1937, and gave himself up.

Charged with first degree murder, Komula was held in a Fergus Falls jail without bail. After a trial, Judge Byron Wilson sentenced Andrew Komula, age 43, to 6 to 30 years in prison for killing Esther Komula, age 32.

News From The Front

Charles Goddard, Company K, 1st Minnesota Volunteer Infantry, was an 18-year-old soldier from Winona who lied his way into the army while he was still 16. Read what he wrote home from the front:

March 26. 1863

My Dear Mother,

Your kind letter dated the 15th of this month I received last evening. For the past two or three days I have not been doing any duty on account of my leg which I sprained. The swelling is down a little maybe. At about this morning the enemy started throwing shells at us. Owing to the peculiar shape of the line they fell fast among us. This we stood until night, with a man falling near us to rise no more. Musketry is one solid roar. The smoke about the combatants shut them from sight and we tried to tell by sound who was retreating. Before sunset we were ordered a short distance to the left and on high ground where we had a full view of the field and its terrible scene. From our front the ground sloped some sixty feet to a ravine.

Then came the order for the division to advance down the slope until we come to the particular spot and then the word CHARGE went down the line. The hill must be held at all costs. Bullets whistled past us, shells, grape shots screeched over us, canister and grape. Comrade after comrade dropped from the ranks right side of us, but on the line went. There was no time to give a fallen friend a look. We had no time to weep. We were nearing the Rebel line and in a moment it will be hand to hand. Two regiments on our right faltered and subjected us to flank fire and we were ordered back, leaving our dead and wounded within a few feet of the Rebel line. Then forward we went again and the Rebs were routed, and the bloody field was in our possession-- but what a cost!! The ground is covered with dead and dying, groans and prayers and cries for help or a drink of water fill the air. The sun has gone down and in the darkness we hurried, stumbled over the field in search of our fallen.

My leg is really hurting. Remember I love you whether I get to say it in person again or not?

Your Charlie

April 5, 1863

Dearest Mother

Your prayers must be helping as I am still on this side of the sod. Not much has changed with me other than I can't put my weight on that leg. Our division was the last reserve and we stacked arms with orders to remain near the stack arms. I think if anybody is getting the worst of it, it is us. Our Division was called in under sharp artillery fire after deploring we laid down where the Rebs shelled rite smart. The order was charge when the two armies were only 500 feet apart. I dropped to the ground with a wounded shoulder. I pulled myself up fast when I seen blood on my shoe the heel of which is tore and I thought it a slight one and run to catch up thinking that we were winning but if not and bayonets had to be used, I wanted a chance at it too. We laid ourselves down now on the ground to get a little rest,

Charles E. Goddard

Alonzo Pickle, Co. K

Capt. Joseph Periam,
Co. K

Gen. Winfield Scott
Hancock, II Corps

we lay sleeping side by side the dead and wounded. Thousands have fallen.

Don't be so foolish as to try and come down here like Mrs. Eli done. You know I said we were under good care with General Winfield Scott Hancock and Captain Periano. As I write I wonder how you will get this. Maybe some day you will. I found another soldier from Winona, Alonzo Pickle. We are heading for tight times. I can only tell you a bit on the edge of it all. We finally got the Humphrey's on the run with Wiocox at their heels heading for a poorly guarded ridge under heavy rifle fire. I am so proud of the First Minnesota Regiment. They deployed the slope..eight companies. They charged headlong down, bayonets fixed, struck the middle of the grey line...already in some disorder as a result of their run of a mile over stony ground. The Confederates recoiled instantly then came again yelling fiercely as they concentrated on one undersized blue regiment.

The result was devastating. Colville and all but three of his officers were killed or wounded, together with 215 of his men. A captain brought the 47 survivors back up the ridge, less than one fifth as many coming down as charged it. Try not to worry mother and stay in good health.

Your loving son, Charles.

Winona in 1861

A Tipsy Saint Nick

The winter of '49 was a cold one with lots of snow. The long driveway up to our farm was a single pair of deep tracks easily blown over. Because of it, my husband was the one who went to Long Prairie once each two weeks with a long list while Larry, his baby brother, and I stayed home. We had managed to get Larry into town the one day Santa visited, so he knew how that grandfatherly Santa behaved.

The year he was five, Larry began the first grade, the only pupil in his grade, in a little country school two miles away. It boasted sixteen students spread over seven grades. Transportation called for a horse and sled twice each school day. "Teacher" was five-foot, two-inch little Miss Moran, fresh out of "Normal School," bent on giving our snowbound little community a memorable Christmas this year. Which she did!

How excited Larry was three weeks before the program, waving a slip of paper that held his "piece." It consisted of one line: "I wish you a Merry Christmas," over and over again. During the next weeks, we practiced until he could have said it in his sleep.

The driveway came in for an extra clearing so we could take the car, making it possible for baby and me to go, too. I looked forward to it as much as Larry did. As the schoolhouse came into view, a respectable-sized plume of white smoke billowed from the chimney into the night sky. A lantern with a red globe sat on the porch to welcome everyone. Candles, stuck in the bottom of fruit jars, shone through each window.

The inside was quite as splendiferous. Two clusters of kerosene lamps in holders attached to the ceiling were all lit (very unusual; they were so hard to reach). Fresh pine boughs scented the air, and green and red paper chains and strings of popcorn crisscrossed the walls. Two bed sheets pinned on wire separated the spectators from the program people.

Excitement and anticipation crackled in the air.

At last snickers and shuffly sounds from behind the curtain died down and Teacher, in a new red dress with a ribbon to match, stepped out to welcome a capacity crowd. She looked proud and pleased.

For the next hour, we watched an assortment of wise men in bedspreads and angels in last year's lace curtains, with Christmas songs in appropriate places. Finally, stepping out from behind the curtain, feet planted well apart, hands behind his back, our Larry proclaimed in a stout voice, "I wish I could marry you all for Christmas over and over again!" He was quite pleased with the crowd's response.

Loud stomping sounds and the jingle of bells could be heard in the entry. It grew quiet, eyes riveted on the doorway. Teacher smiled broadly at her surprise. She hadn't promised a Santa because she

wasn't sure she could talk her brother-in-law into the job.

"Whoa, Pransher, whoa, Vixshon," and the door burst open to reveal Santa in all his glory. It was easily twenty degrees below zero and a blast of it came with him through the door. His cap had slid backward, his pillow-stomach rested just under his chin, and his whiskers started from under one ear. None of this dampened his spirits. "It'sh mighty cold for ole Shanta Claush, waitin' all thish time. Had to keep warm shomehow," he confided to some of the men. Car heaters in those days were in name only.

Teacher stood to one side, hands clenched, eyes blazing. She considered her program ruined. And this, her very first one! About that time Santa spotted her, making an erratic path over to plant a loud juicy kiss that landed in front of her ear as she ducked. "Now, now, cute li'l teasher, you're too part(hick!)iklar. Whyn't you shend out shome coffee to ole Shanty Slaush? It wa'sh cold!"

As he bumbled around the room, running into desks, asking each child, "Shay, have you been good?" Parents, no matter how incensed we'd been at first, were roaring with the kids. Even stiff-necked Miss Whitney, on the school board, was smiling.

As the warmth penetrated, Santa became louder and happier, falling flat when he tried a little soft-shoe shuffle. It was hilarious! Finally, two of the men each grabbed an arm and propelled him out the door and home. He left yelling, "Merry Chrishmash, ever' body!" over his shoulder. I took little Teacher in a corner, dried her eyes and assured her the program had been lovely (even if our kid did want to marry them all for Christmas) and it HAD been a long wait in a cold car for Santa; the parents understood. It wasn't her fault.

It was quiet in the car on the way home. Then, sticking his elbows over the back of the front seat, Larry asked in a tentative tone, "Mom, didn't you think that Santa Claus acted sort of, well--sort of kinda funny? I didn't think Santa Claus talked like that, either--did you Dad?"

"Yeah, I guess we could say he was a little different.. Likely never see another one just like him." I knew Dad was smiling as he tried to stay in one deep track.

Since that Christmas so long ago, Larry can't count the Santas he's seen, plus the dozens he's taken his children to see.

But, the only one he remembers, that stands out, is that one of so long ago, who didn't seem quite right, somehow.

Oscar's Hair Froze Down

Making a new life for a family in a foreign country was easier said than done Oscar was finding out. He left Sweden, where the rich got rich and the poor could go jump in the Atlantic. Oscar heard a Swede who was just back for a visit to talk about his new life. Oscar liked what he heard. In just five weeks Oscar and Anna, Herman and Katrina, five and eight years old were on their way in a sailboat for America. It took three weeks. Their first stop was a little town near Chicago. After a season, Anna talked Oscar into moving to St. Paul, where she had a cousin. All of the families cooked on the same stove.

Oscar counted himself lucky to get road work on the railroad between St. Paul and Lake Superior. They got into big timber that had to be cut down to make a road wide enough for two-yoke ox teams to get through with a load on skids. Provisions were stacked 10 and 12 miles apart. Sixty-three men were to clear a mile in a day. It was hard work, but paid more than it would have in Sweden. Working overtime paid double. They were issued tin plates and were served from a cook wagon, usually pork, beef, and dried peas and beans. No bunk houses were built as they never camped overnight in the same place twice.

Snowbanks took the place of chairs. They had to eat with mittens on. Oscar did not look forward to night when they tramped down a patch in a snowdrift big enough to make a bed. Pine branches were spread over the snow a foot deep, if possible. A blanket was thrown over it and they climbed in to try for sleep. A blanket was fastened over the top to make like a tent. It was purely miserable in every way, they all agreed. They slept in heavy coats and boots. A side effect none welcomed were the infestation of lice that moved in on their bodies. For convenience and warmth most men sported long hair and whiskers, that often froze down and had to be chopped loose in the morning.

One of the men caught cold and they left him with a fur trader, where he died. Thieves followed them like vultures, crooks knew when they were paid. Oscar liked the lay of the land around St. Paul. When the ice was gone they visited a cousin in Red Wing. Oscar's family decided to move in with them until a cabin was built.

Before the soddy was made livable, twins were born in a covered wagon. They were named Sophia and David and both died close together. Friends carried them in their arms the 10 miles to a real cemetery. Oscar chopped wood that first winter. He had to go 30 miles, leaving his family with only a half sack of flour and a little corn. It took a week to get to Sioux Falls. There were only two homesteads the entire way.

In 1888, the Dakotas, Minnesota, Nebraska, and Kansas suffered a terrible blizzard. The day started out to be a fine spring day but by afternoon dark clouds loaded with moisture filled the sky. The snow came down heavily as the temperature dropped farther down than thermometers were marked. Many got lost and froze to death. In the spring, frozen cattle were standing on high pillars of snow and ice. That spring the river was a mile wide with waves.

During this time, Oscar and Anna were in Sioux Falls. They stayed until the storm was over, then drove slowly from Sioux Falls across the country over snow drifts that had buried four-feet-high fences. The horses lunged ahead breaking though, then sinking down to rest.

Oscar would gather his family together on Sunday afternoon and read a sermon for that Sunday. He sent for books he thought would help him. Oscar was a deeply spiritual and Christian man. They became property owners by practicing persistence, faith, hard work, and optimism for the future.

Why'd You Do That, Pa?

"Nineteen-fifty, I got nineteen-fifty and who'll say twenty? Hey, folks, you ain't lookin' at this horse right! Only seven years old, nice an' steady. Shucks, blind as a bat, but gettin' your old lady to lead her will take care of that. Who says twenty?'

"Twenty!" yelled Pa. A titter rose from the crowd.

"They're laughin' at us Pa. Why'd you do that?" Charlie let his head drop and kicked a rock. Hanna, younger than Charlie by three years, dropped Pa's hand.

Pa elbowed through the crowd to claim his blind horse while the others jeered. "Think you can get Annie to lead'er all the way to Kansas?" "Lookout she don't step on you or fall in a hole," another voice said. Charlie and Hanna melted toward the back of the crowd.

Pa tied the horse to the back of the wagon and climbed on the high seat. They rode in silence. "I don't like to be laughed at," Hanna said in a small voice from between Pa and Charlie.

"I know, kids. Just you wait. They'll be laughing out the sides of their mouths pretty soon. You'll see."

Ma was on the stoop when they drove in the yard. She took one look at the horse's eyes with the white spots in them, gave Pa a long level look and went in the house. The door slammed. Hinges jumped.

Hanna put the pillow over her head that night after the lights were out. She was sick of Ma and Pa's arguing after they thought the kids were asleep. She had a bellyful of hearing about land for fifty cents an acre. And, what did "prove it up" mean? Pa did most of the talkin'. Ma mostly cried.

Both made lists on what to take along. Ma's were longer than Pa's, but what he wrote down stayed. More'n half of Ma's was crossed out. Loading time came. Pa tied on a keg of nails, Ma brought a sack of dried beans. Pa added seed corn, Ma came with a chair wrapped in a blanket.

"Sorry, Annie, but we ain't goin' to have room for that."

"No room for my chair? It was a wedding present. My pa made it outta hickory." Tears were spilling down her cheeks again. Then she straightened up, dried her eyes, and set the chair firmly in the wagon. "The chair goes or I don't!"

"I'll make you a real handsome bench first thing, honey. Honest."

Ma never took her eyes off Pa, nor unloaded the chair. Pa looked beat.

The wagon train pulled out the next morning with 12 wagons. Tears were shed since, likely, they'd never meet again. All the talk among the men was how wide and deep the big river they had to cross would be at this time of year. After three days of travel, they heard the roar of it a full day before they got there. Three wagon drivers looked and turned back. Hanna wished Pa would, too. Mosquitoes were like a dark cloud. They got in ears, eyes, everywhere, and about drove the horses crazy.

It was early Monday that Amos Kicker, wagon master, said there was no use to wait. The river wasn't gonna go away. He told the women not to worry, hitched tandem style, that's one team ahead of the other on each wagon, they should have plenty of power.

"I'll lead the way, seein' as how my horses are the biggest. If we can get one team to go the rest likely will follow." Amos gave the harness one more checking, climbed aboard and braced his feet. He drove to where the bank slanted and lined up his lead team. Then, with a slap of the reins, roared "Giddyap, come on Prince, Queenie, get a goin'. Hey, hey, hey, dig in!"

It didn't work. The boiling boisterous river terrified them. Heads high, eyes rolling white, they tried to turn first one way and then the other, parallel to the river. Next, the lead team split, each going a different direction. Tore the harness to smithereens. After he got them calmed down, Amos said "I don't think we're goin' to make it, boys. Have to try this fall when the river's down."

Pulling out of line, Pa said in his quiet way, "Care if I try it?" Ma went as white as a sheet. She

held Charlie and Hanna tight.

Nobody noticed Pa had hitched his big stallion and the gelding as the wheel team, putting a sturdy mare and the blind horse in the lead. Amos pulled his rig out of the way, looked at Pa like his gears was slippin', an' said, "Sure. Go to it."

Pa pulled up to the water's edge of the river. He talked soft to his horses, then gave a whoop and a yell with a hard slap of the line on the blind horse's behind. Surprised, she took a mighty lunge that landed her a full length into the water, pulling the others with her. The wheel team had no choice but to follow and pull.

Others lined up and came with various degrees of success. The horses had to swim the middle channel while people prayed the wagons would float and didn't turn sideways. A good thing the river wasn't a little wider. A little ways down Pa's team clambered up a slippery bank, winded. The other wagons came floundering after as best they could. Everybody made it, somehow. The Campbell's lost a crate of layin' hens. A hump-back trunk floated away from somebody. Tubs and pans that had been hung on the outside got away. Everything had to be dried out.

Pa busied himself with the harness, trying not to look pleased, like he did it every day. Just the same, he was praised and back-slapped. "How'd you ever think of hitchin' yor horses thataway?" Amos asked.

"Figures, don't it? A blind horse can't see what she's gettin' into until it's too late. I jest kept'em movin'. Been searchin' for a blind horse since last spring. Bound to be some places a seein' horse wouldn't want to go." Pa tried not to smile.

Ma slipped up to Pa, sayin', "I'll be right proud if you can find time to make me a settin' bench." Pa nodded, he was busy talkin' baby-talk to his horses.

Hanna and Charlie each hung on one of his hands. He was their Pa.

Squatting down to their level, Pa put an arm around each one. "You see, kids, just cause something is wrong with a critter don't mean he ain't good for anything." Hanna kind of knew he meant people, too.

Hanna was 90 years old and a resident of Shady Lane Nursing Home in Wadena, Minnesota, when she told this story. She never forgot it.

Diana Lucina Spicer Block

Submitted by Gail Coutts....Notable women ancestors series. http://www.rootsweb.com/~block.html

Diana was born on a sunny day April 23, 1868. She lived in Evanston, Wyoming, with her mother and a new stepfather, four stepbrothers and a stepsister. She met Albert Block the first time when she was 12 and he was 18. Albert reappeared when she was 18. He married and in due time two little girls were born. Diana was their baby-sitter sometimes. After two years of marriage, he divorced his wife. Diana was 14 by then. When she was 17, he came back with courting on his mind. In 1887, when she was 18, they were married.

In Diana's words, "Albert worked on the railroad and made good wages. Our first child was Bill, born in Evanston on March 23, 1888. A year later all our belongings went into a wagon and we moved to Ogden, Utah. Albert truly liked to travel. About the only places he didn't want to take a look at were the Dakotas and Minnesota. They were just too durned cold, from what he had heard."

A year later, they loaded all their belongings into a covered wagon and moved to Idaho Falls where an sister of Diana's father lived. Albert took out a homestead of 160 acres. Albert cleared land and worked in the grist mill that ground flour.

There was an Indian uprising that winter with 150 Blackfeet on the warpath. They were on the other side of the Snake River. They could be seen burning one farm after the other. Many innocent homesteaders lost their lives. Albert joined the Home Guard and helped quiet them time and again. He took the children and Diana to the fort. It was a fearful job getting through the snow. When they drew closer to the fort they were mistaken for Indians, who played that trick, until someone recognized Albert. Diana and the children stayed for three weeks at the fort.

Diana Lucina Spicer Block
ca. 1913

Albert came back with a scar of a bullet across the back of his neck. He enjoyed showing the scar.

A big Indian buck stepped out of the trees when Sister Lucy visited Diana. They were resting in the shade...and there he was. They were so scared, but he only wanted food. There was a big pot of beans that were sour. They were to go to the pigs. He saw it and started to eat. He finished it and started to whoop and holler and dance around. Diana was sure he was sick, then he went off laughing into the woods. They never saw him again. Diana thought he had the bellyache. They never knew who would ride in. One day three men on horseback stopped. One had a wounded hand. His thumb was just hanging. He asked Diana to fix it. When she told him she had nothing to put on it he took axle grease from the barn and spread it all over. She bandaged it up and

sewed it on with black thread. When Albert came home that night his first words were, I saw a terrible sight. There were three men hanging from a tree. One had his hand bandaged. It turned out they were on stolen horses. Albert always teased Diana for doctoring a horse thief.

Diana had a pair of twins in 1891 and nearly died. The day started out fine and Albert went to work. All went well until Diana lifted on a heavy pail of water, then the pains started. She managed to get back into the cabin before she passed out. She came around when she saw her mother and brother from Idaho Falls were helping her. They saved her life. Both babies smothered to death before her mother arrived. Lucy was born the next year, while Diana was still in a run down condition. The doctor said the climate in Oregon was healthier, so Albert let the government claim go back and loaded up the wagon.

They met a family by the name of Davis at American Falls who were in trouble. Mrs. David was about to have a baby and Mr. Davis was blinded by poison ivy. Their stock, including the horses, had run away. The Block's could not leave them like that so they stayed. It was September and Albert knew they had to hurry and get over the mountains. They followed the old Immigrant Trail. What a long hard trip it turned out to be. Food and water had to be planned ahead. Money ran out so Albert sold a treasured gold watch as well as anything else worth something. Real suffering was about to set in.

It was November and settlements were far between. For the first time Albert was worried. It was a dry cold. Early winter storms were coming. Mrs. Davis was going to have her baby soon. Seeing cattle grazing lifted their spirits as people must be near. If one of the cattle had been killed for food the penalty was hanging. Each day came along worse. The day a cowboy rode over the hill and into camp was a God send! He told them there was a big camp six days ahead. They knew they could not hold out another six days without help The cowboy told them to kill a beef. They did, ate too much and were too sick to travel for the next several days. They just got started when Mrs. David went into labor. She was desperately

sick for many hours, with no help. Diana did not know what to do. The water was gone.

Two or three days later in a very bad way, they pulled in at the ranch. Camp was hastily set up and Albert went to the house for help. The foreman said they had no supplies that would help, but they would not go hungry. There was plenty of water. They said camping overnight would be fine, but they would have to move on the next day. Albert was heartsick. He knew they would never make Santa Rosa without help. Alfred hated to tell the rest the bad news. He did not know that while he was gone a bunch of cowboys had seen them and stopped by...They had never seen a newborn baby before.

Diana and Mrs. Davis could not believe Alfred's news, that the rancher would not let them take food, how would the children live? That evening in drooping spirits they sat around the campfire. When a foreman heard about the baby he filled two big wheelbarrows with grub and was bringing it out. Again, they wanted to see the baby. One cowboy passed his hat for the new baby and got quite a few dollars. In another few days they started out. The baby died three months later. They limped into Santa Rosa just before Christmas. They had traveled 1000 miles in three and a half months. Money was gone and almost no food. The good ladies from a church brought a wonderful dinner.

Albert soon found work and made $10 a week. George was born in 1894, just before Albert was made a partner in the second-hand store where he worked. In the next two years they saved enough to buy a home. Diana was happier here than she had ever been. In 1896 Eve came two months too early and weighed three pounds. She was so weak. They made a kind of incubator for her out of a box padded with cotton, and placed her between two bats. Bottles of hot water kept her warm. She was too weak so Diana fed her with a medicine dropper filled with milk squeezed from her own breasts.

Diana saw Albert turning itchy again and dreaded the day he would want to move. For the first time she had a home and regular food coming in. Eve was six months old when he said they were

heading for Gold Hill, Oregon. Diana cried. Then a letter said Diana's mother and step-father were going to try gold mining and wanted Diana and Alfred to go along. Alfred was happy, so they all met at Red Bluffs and traveled together to Rogue River where they made camp. The men set up a gold mine and found little gold for their hard work. The family suffered from cold and hunger, enduring many hardships. Diana couldn't think about the home she had to give up without crying. Besides, she was pregnant again. They saved enough to get them over the mountains to Crescent City, where Clara was born in 1898 in a company house that belonged to the sawmill where Albert worked.

The older Block children were old enough to go to school, but they had almost no clothing. When a teacher found out what was keeping them home she brought a big bag of bleached flour sacks. Diana made them all kinds of garments by hand. Bill hated his bleached flour sack pants. They stayed in Crescent City four years. Albert left the mill and bought a saloon. They made the most money and Albert liked it. Diana did not like the life. Albert was coming home in great spirits those nights. Diana said if he didn't get out of it she would burn it down. He believed her and sold out. They moved to Waldo, Oregon, to take out another claim. Frank was born there in 1902.

Alfred always got restless in the spring and, sure enough, he bought a photography tent and camera and traveled all summer from town to town taking pictures. Diana was happy to stay on the ranch. She enjoyed a neighbor close enough when Albert was gone. Then the Block children got sick with small pox. Pest houses were built, it was such an epidemic. Sick people were supposed to either die or be kept alone. With much prayer and God's help, the children were well before Albert came back. He was tired of taking pictures and wanted to move again.

They moved back to Crescent City to stay with Diana's folks with all of their kids. In the spring they headed down the coast to Sonoma County. In Cloverdale Albert got a contract to strip tan bark off trees in the mountains. He hired men to help as it was hard work. This kind of bark was used in tanning hides and they were there over a year. Diana cooked for the men and her own big family. It was early spring when she knew for sure there was another baby on the way. The summer of 1904 was a hard one, hot and dry. When she knew her time was close she got Albert to get a real doctor to be there. She waited too long and went into labor. The pains got worse with every turn of the wheels. On the banks of the Russian River near Heraldsburg, Albert pitched the tent. The children were worried to see their mother that sick. Eve and Clara tried to make her feel better by bringing two big pears they picked off a tree. She told them to put the pears on her pillow and run to bed. In the morning they would find another brother or sister. During the night Albert, with Bill and May's help, delivered a baby named Ruby. They stayed in that camp two weeks before they moved on.

In the spring Albert found five acres in Elverano. There was a little cabin and an orchard. They used the last money for a down payment. There was no water. Albert and the older children worked for ranches, picking potatoes, hops, and grapes. Diana kept busy canning fruit. Albert built bunk beds along the end of the cabin, dug a well and put up a windmill. Then came a small barn and a cow. He started a house, with Diana's help. She kept more than busy with a garden, planting fruit trees and a yard with flowers. A loud rumble in the morning of April, 1906, brought them to their feet. A gust of wind slammed a door open, the cabin was shaking and the windmill was going in circles. It was a quake that destroyed San Francisco 50 miles away.

Diana tried to hurry the building of the new house in order to have a bedroom ready for a new baby. This was the home of her dreams. It had 2 big bedrooms with more planned, a bath, a large kitchen and pantry. Erving was born there in November of 1906. When he was a year old Albert heard about the railroad building a spur to a big coal mine going through Stone Canyon. The Blocks needed money, so they closed up their home and went. Albert was hired as a foreman. He rented a house for Diana and the kids. In 1908 Carl was born and they moved to

Chancellor, where Diana was hired to run a boarding house for a hundred men. She cleaned and cooked every minute of every day. The children helped. They were really not old enough but they needed the money.

They moved back to Elverano and Albert got a job in a lumber mill. A year later the stepfather died and Diana's mother was alone. Diane felt needed so she headed for Crescent City. The stage driver turned out to be one of Bill's school friends. Early that evening dark clouds gathered. Midnight found them at the halfway station. They changed horses and started out again. Soon, it started to really storm. It was too dark to see the road so the driver dropped the lines and the horses found their own way. It was a fearful night that ended the next day in Crescent City. Diana's mother was too sick to leave so it was decided to bring her to Block's place. The first automobile stage was making it in three weeks. Diana decided to wait for it.

It turned out to be a worse trip instead of easier. The drivers were not experienced at driving over steep narrow roads. Passengers had to walk around each sharp curve. There was a peck of walking! When Diana's mother was too sick, men carried her. She settled into Diana's family fine. There was always work to be done. When they put family and supplies in the wagon once each summer and headed for the hops and grape orchards it was like a picnic. On that trip Albert and the kids made enough to buy winter clothes. It was during this time that Bill and May were married. Besides working in the lumber yard, Albert took over the movie house. It was called the "Elverano Villa". He showed movies three times a week. A cart with a sign announced the movie. With the kids holding the sign the cart went slowly up and down the streets.

Diana found life easier these days. Older children helped with younger ones. Bill had a good job and sent money home. Albert was doing fair and seemed settled. Even so, every few months he would take on a "gold finding" trip, taking the money and coming back broke. He was forever on a big money deal and ready to take off. He often took some of the children along. They were often cold and hungry, looking like ragged orphans, still they wanted to go with him. It left them great stories to tell, some fantastic true things. At last, Diana had a nice yard with flowers and vegetables. She loved to see her children gathering around Albert to hear one of his great true stories. Winter nights they spent time around the stove, singing, while she mended from her rocker and sewing basket.

The peace and quiet did not last. Terrible screams came one night from the kitchen, which was a mass of flames. Clara was screaming. Thinking she was on fire, Diana fainted. Grandma had tipped the lantern over, spilling oil all over herself. She was a living torch and started to run. Albert ripped her clothes off and wrapped her in a blanket. She was terribly burned. The flesh fell from her breasts and cords in her neck tightened and almost choked her. Diana sat with her mother night and day. Nothing helped. The doctor came every day. Diana would go to the chicken coop and get fresh eggs still warm. With tweezers the doctor dropped tiny pieces of the soft skin inside the shell on the open burns. The skin would start to grow. After many months she started to heal but she never recovered from the shock. She was always a care until she died in 1929.

By this time Diana was over forty years old. Clara had married and Albert and Diana had six grandchildren. With a shock, Diana realized that she was pregnant again! She was heartsick. Albert felt bad for Diana...but thought a baby would be wonderful. He said "This one will be a great comfort in our old age." Maxwell, the eleventh child, was born April 24, 1916, one day after Diana was 47. When she held him in her arms the first time, she asked God to let her live to raise him. Her prayers were answered. His nick name was "Chubby". He was a blessing as were all of the rest. Before Chubby was born the owner of the lumber yard died. Albert thought it a good investment. He talked Diana into mortgaging their home to buy it. It only took a few months before Albert knew it was a bad deal and they lost their home. It was a terrible blow to Diana. She had friends, now.

She had worked so hard. But, it was done. No use to look back so she got ready to move again.

Albert turned back to the railroad. He could speak either Mexican or Chinese so he was sent to Los Angeles to run a section gang. They all moved along except Bill. This time they were moved on a boat called "Rose City". This new adventure took three days. Nobody wanted to rent a house to such a big family. One was rented on the edge of town. They were asked to move after a time. Their boys were so wild and destructive being cooped up. They needed a place where they could hunt, fish and have jobs. Running expenses were high here. With no chickens or garden, ends did not meet. Then a way opened up.

Diana's step father had been a veteran in the Civil War. His wife, Diana's mother, had applied for a widows pension and been accepted. She got a back pay check for $500 and gave it to Diana to buy a home with. Blocks went to East Los Angeles because it was a new part being developed. The new home on Bonnie Beach was just right. They had chickens, a pig, and a garden. The country life for the boys was most important. They soon had swimming holes, fishing streams, rabbit trails, and friends. They were fairly settled when Albert felt a gold mining trip coming on. Diana warned him that she would not leave this home. He could go any time, anywhere, stay as long as he liked but she had finished moving. As years passed Albert's trips became fewer and shorter. He stayed with the railroad until the depression when he was laid off. He never went back.

Eve and Lucy went into obstetrics training in a hospital. One of their new friends was Emma Hurd. She spent many a weekend at the Blocks. Now unmarried again, Bill decided to join the family in 1917 to celebrate his mother's birthday. Bill and Emma fell in love at first sight. She loved and was loved by every member of the family. Bill was drafted, made a machine gunner and sent to Siberia where his luck ran out. Lucy lost her husband with influenza in 1919. She and her Billie came home to live.

In 1923 they built a small cabin where the garden had been. They could no longer have livestock so Albert built Diana a bird aviary there. She enjoyed raising Canaries and a good strain of German Rollers. Diana soon had a business built up. The Block children were all married by this time. In the 1930's hard times started, one by one the boys lost their jobs. They all moved closer to home and ate at the same table. That made 21 for each meal. By 1934 everyone had found work again and things were normal. George was killed by a stray bolt of lightening in 1926. It was a shock, but an act of God and you did not doubt the Lord.

In 1937 a grand Golden Wedding Anniversary was celebrated in Montebelle Park. Friends came from near and far.

※※

It was 1941, Mother Block leaned back in her chair, saying "I have told you how I had my children. Now, I want to tell you how I lost them."

I, Devonna Bezzant Block, listened while memories crowded each other in this home where death was no stranger, indeed: Carl died in 1941, Bill in 1942, Frank in 1943, Albert in 1944, May in 1945, and Lucy in 1953. All of these deaths broke Diana's heart, but not her faith in God. She said, "I knew when He gave them to me they would only be mine until He wanted them back."

Diana Lucina Spicer Block celebrated her 104th birthday April 23, 2002.

Bogs, Bridges and Bugs

I signed my name, Christen E. Borge, on the document and took off to see what kind of real estate I had bought. This meant leaving Coon Prairie for Lake Park, Wisconsin. We bid not only our friends good-bye, but everything we knew. Like Horace Greely demanded of young men, we went west into a completely unknown environment. On October 20, 1850, we started out, my family and me, with many well wishers to see us off.

I didn't expect the team of huge oxen I'd bought would take right to it like old times, nor did I expect them to overturn everything into a deep ditch and break the wagon tongue, which they did without a thought. Sometimes they plodded along like veterans in the single track, the next they ran side of it. My arms ached by night. We camped at La Crosse that night, cold and discouraged, to eat a scant supper and crawl into our blankets.

The next day things looked brighter, especially after I found out that there was a ferry and I wouldn't have to try to swim those characters I'd bought across. There were other dangers awaiting us, as I found out when I wanted those lummoxes to back up a few feet. They backed in a grand flourish toward a 100 foot drop straight into the Mississippi River. A protruding rock behind one wheel is all that saved us from plunging down into a wildly boiling current. The river was majestic, a heavy wild thing more devil than angel. Sometimes it was one; often the other. The bottom was carpeted with rigs whose drivers hadn't paid attention to the voice of the river on its rambunctious way to the gulf. We had to unload everything to make it to the top of a steep hill. Another wagon with a more reliable source of power saw our predicament and pulled us up to the top where, after walking everything up, we reloaded again. We looked back from the summit to bid LaCrosse goodbye with little regret.

Ours was a slow tiresome journey because poor forage with little nutrition in it did not give our oxen needed strength. We rested them often. We finally arrived in Otter Tail City in June. We ran into Martin Olson returning from Becker County to fetch his family. He gave us a picture of that part of the country like it was a little hunk of real estate dropped to earth from Heaven above to become Becker County. Of course, we said we'd take a look at it.

Martin somehow forgot to mention that only Indian trails traveled to Otter Tail City. Nothing that resembled a road went that way. On one end of Becker County we had to cross a wicked swamp. It was the culprit that caused many hardships in loss of strength for both man and beast. In that low country mosquitoes drove our animals wild. Our kids were covered with welts, as were we. The swamp encompassed many acres. There was no way we could see around it, and we couldn't get through it. That left only finding some way to build a bridge. Everyone set to work with that in mind.

The first ones got across fine, but the "bridge," as we called it, deteriorated badly until the last wagons and teams had to be pulled out. Finally, we were across.

Once on the other side we scattered. We were rid of the slough and were among big trees. We chose Section 8, on June 20, 1870. The shanty we threw together before anything else was done, was 10 feet by 12 feet with a 7 foot wide ridge in the middle. We gave it a cord wood roof like we did the road, and found out as soon as it rained that our roof hardly stopped the rain from coming straight down. The inside was a slippery mess. The flat "bed" was made from a couple of oak poles 3 feet long laid 6 feet apart and covered with poles. We had no table so we used a box we had packed in. Stools were made from heavy chunks of oak with a bit of limb left on for handles. They were immensely clumsy. For tools we had one old ax with a chipped head.

We broke a few acres ready to plant in 1870, which was seeded in 1871. Grasshoppers moved in and moved us out. We didn't get a single grain. We had held back a sack of seed to replant in '72, which

we did. A fair crop came in 1874. In 1875, the hoppers were back in such numbers as to ditch railroad trains because the rails were so slippery with their bodies. That year was our Waterloo. We as well as most of our neighbors hung up farming and went to work laying track for the railroad.

During all of these years the Indians had been pestiferous, burning hay stacks, stealing cattle and horses. In 1870, when Gunder Olsen went out to a burning stack, they shot him in the back. Another family by the name of Johnson were all killed in '72. A family of five went next. Indians donning war paint were dancing the war dance wildly on the White Earth Reservation. There was a white minister on the reservation who warned the whites at Lake Park. A fort was built and leaders carefully chosen. There would be extensions put on the fort from the inside. Railroad ties were set upright in ditches with port holes on all sides. Women and children were brought inside. Men were made sentinels. Everyone remained here for a week. Cattle left at home had to forage for themselves.

To everyone's relief, Indians on the warpath did not show up, thanks to the minister who had been working with them. Thanks to these early denizens of the county, Becker County pioneers prevailed.

Trapped At Race Rocks

More than 15 ships lay scattered on the bottom among boulders two fathoms deep off the coast of Vancouver Island, British Columbia, Canada. The first recorded victim, the French ship, Nanette. She went down just three days before the lights were turned on during Boxing Day 1860.

Race Rocks, named for the swift tide flow in the channel one mile from Rocky Point on Vancouver Island, claimed more than her share of victims, even after the light house was built cooperatively by England and the United States. The Biddle went under in 1867, the Sword Fish in 1877, the Rosedale in 1882, and the Castle in 1886.

Living conditions on the rock were far from ideal. It was always damp and chilly. Tragedy seemed to follow the families who operated the lights. On Christmas Day 1865 the lighthouse keeper's wife's brother, his wife, and three friends lost their lives only 50 feet from shore, within sight of the lighthouse family. At that time, there was no boat on shore.

As is the case with most modern lighthouses, Race Rocks Lighthouse is now automated.

John Walter Potter

In the hands of Indians, the archaic bow and arrow became a formidable weapon. Army surgeons in the 1880's were challenged by them beyond their scope of knowledge. All of a doctor's ingenuity was called upon when removing an arrow head from a deep wound, too often followed by gushing blood.

Dr. Gray was an army surgeon whose territory was the Dakotas in the 1860's. On June 3, 1869, the company H, 22nd Infantry was in the front lines. One soldier's skull was penetrated two inches by an arrow. He was anesthetized with chloroform before a Hey's Saw began chewing its way through his skull until they reached the arrow head. Following the operation he was told to rest, eat a low-calorie diet, elevate his head and apply saline cathartics. He was back in active duty in 4 days.

When I (John Walter Potter) was 18 years old in 1889, the Indians were upset because the settlers were killing too much game. Sitting Bull was leading the Sioux against the settlers. I heard of the request for volunteers while on my way going through Minneapolis. Since I loved to hold a gun, I signed up with a large group of rookies. They needed soldiers and I was big and strong so they told me to lie about my age.

First the Sargent marched us to the doctor's office, then to a restaurant. Finally, they got enough men to fill a train and we were shipped west. The train was headed for Bismarck, North Dakota. A soldier I knew related all the bad things with army life. My parents did not know I had enlisted until he told them.

The soldiers were out drilling so it was quiet when we arrived. The food was really poor and we were always hungry. When the mess hall bell sounded we all broke formation and ran for the dining hall. It made our Sargent really angry so we never did that again. Fort Abraham Lincoln held the 12th and 22nd Infantries. I was assigned to a company that was a part of the 7th Cavalry and two detached units. Our

Potter's Parents

captain was Iprine and the adjutant was A. Sharp. I was assigned to teaching the children on the base.

I liked teaching. There were not many jobs in the army like that. I was in charge of four rooms. Another soldier taught the soliders what they had missed in grade school, except when they were needed to help fight Indians. I liked being boss. The soldiers didn't amount to much the day after pay day. If they saw a movie with animals in it, the next few days they went around sounding like that animal. It was crazy.

There were many Indians who came through. Many Indian braves were wearing white men's pants. The Indians loved to gamble. We would shoot at targets. They were good with arrows. They would gamble anything, stones or whatever. They would toss a spear as far as they could, run pick it up and toss it again. The first one to cross a line was the winner. We called their game "long tennis".

Our pay was $13.00 a month. They kept back $4 each time to give it when we got out. They gave

us food, but tobacco and other items had to be bought. It didn't take long to spend $9.00. Ft. Abraham was on the Mississippi Rover. Winters were very cold and long. We would be sawing wood and a blizzard would come up so fast we had to run to the fort a half-mile away. By that time our ears and nose would be frozen. The lads who could take it best came from Minnesota. One of my best buddies was Gustav Pohl, a farmer from Minnesota who liked the cold. One fellow had never fired a gun and did not know how to handle a fire arm. He did not know a Springfield had a 90 pound recoil kick back so he held it inches away from his shoulder. He got a sore shoulder. The next time he put padding under his shirt, then the Captain found it and gave him 40 more rounds of ammunition to shoot.

Soldiering was quite a game. I enjoyed it. I kept my brass and shoes shined. I made some good friends. General Custer had a theater built at Ft. Abraham and the soldiers put on plays, some of them were real actors. They were so good the wives were invited to see it. We had a gymnasium, too. Many soldiers were heavy drinkers. They would go into Mandan to get whiskey. One time several soldiers who got leave went in to pick up booze for the rest. They got as far as the outskirts of town and passed out. The winters were extremely cold for even the Minnesota guys. The army issued us buffalo coats. A fellow from Mandan built a shack across the river and stocked it with whiskey and a couple of girls. His joint was always busy. One afternoon a couple of us went to the shack. He had a bar keep who was a good story teller. While he was wrapped up talking we were putting bottles of beer in our buffalo coats.

After almost five years the war was over. While I enjoyed the comrades I found in the army the sad fact was too many of them didn't come home. My last job was to help dismantle the fort. From now on all the forts were open.

Railroad Trestle Trouble

Great was our delight when an outside pastor or priest came to hold services. We eagerly selected our best linen to fashion an altar in our house, decorating it with flowers and candles. Everyone attended these services. Good Bishop Ireland, not knowing many of our people came from Holland, sent priests who spoke only the English language. Many of the women were homesick to confess in their native tongue.

One day, having received an invitation from a German-speaking priest in Granite Falls, many happy women and children started out in a big new wagon under the guidance of an elderly newcomer. We waited for their return all afternoon and at dusk, when they had still not appeared, we became alarmed. Some of us walked out in the direction from which they should come.

To our surprise we found the wagon on a railroad trestle with the horses' feet dangling between the cross ties. We flagged down the approaching train and everyone helped get the wagon and horses back on solid ground. When we asked the driver why he drove onto the trestle, he replied "I--I thought American horses were trained to walk on that queer kind of a bridge!"

A Northern Pacific engine, photographed in 1870.

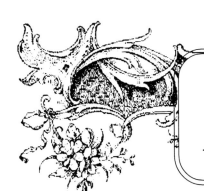

Tie Your Shoes Around Your Neck

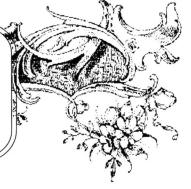

We--James and Margaret Strang--left Glasgow, never to return, on April 29, 1873. Our itinerary took us from Quebec up the St. Lawrence River, dodging huge chunks of ice, to Superior. The precarious voyage took 21 weeks. From there we went to Brainerd. There was no place to stay so we went back to the railroad company and told them. They had reception houses along the line and hauled us to a fine homey place. I stayed there for a time while James went to Alexandria to file on our claim.

After going to Wadena to look up our land, we walked 60 miles through the woods. We followed a blaze line through Parkers Prairie where we made some good friends, then to the Alexandria to the land office, after we got the papers we walked back to Parkers Prairie. We were tired and rested there with the storekeeper. We finally got together a cow and calf, chickens, and general household supplies. Two other families we came with on the boat stayed at the reception house in Brainerd until our men came for us. The Indians were having a big pow wow in the woods. We could hear their yells and see the smoke; we didn't know anything about them as we never got that kind of news in the homeland. Then one night the most unearthly yells broke out. We fastened the door up tight and slept upstairs. We were badly scared, as we looked out the window to see if fate was loose on us. Mrs. Hurst, our hostess came into our room, saying "Mrs. Strang and Mrs. Stewart, say your prayers for our last hour has come."

I said "No! The Lord of heaven will not let them kill us! Be still and know that the Lord knows our predicament." The Indians were busy putting wood up all round the house to burn us out. During this time the dear Lord was putting it in the hearts of the officers at Brainerd to help these helpless women and children. I went to the windows and there was a row of fine strapping chaps were standing with their rifles cocked, who said, "We will shoot you down like dogs," in Indian talk. Say, they turned tail and ran right over each other in a rush to get away. We knelt and thanked the Lord. Then, I said "Let's go down and thank these dear men for our safety." We could say no more. The boys could understand. I lived that day over and over, even if it was fifty years ago, it turned my hair gray. I was only 20 years old.

It was June 17, 1873, in late afternoon. We had not even a tent to go to, but the sun was still high. Wild flowers were everywhere and so brilliant. The sun glinted on them in many colors. We went to the "Strang Place". Loren Langley took us with his team. Our cattle and supplies were at his father's place since we did not know where we were going. We stopped in at a little shanty of logs. It was Nels Roland's place. We were glad to stay for the night. The mosquitoes were so thick you could cut them with a knife. The little house was full of them. The logs were so open you could have thrown a cat through. And how it lightening and thundered! Our trunks and boxes were all outdoors. We had to lift our beds off the floor as we were flooded out. We put Mrs. Stewart's children up on the table, and for the rest of the night we worked out plans to build our houses. Bright and early the next day we were on our feet and got lumber to build and get started.

Jack Stewart and Mr. Strang started to drill a well. We got down about 20 feet and there was plenty of water, but it proved not to account for much. It did for the time being. Then we all got into building

the house to get us all into, until the other one was up and then we each had our own homes. The Stewarts were always good friends. That summer stands out as the most really homesick times that a homesick girl ever had. I would sit by the hour and think of the dear ones left home. My mother and father were gone to their Lang Alma, but my brother, Andrew, has been both. He filled their place for us. He was good and kind, and he did the best he knows how. Now, I was married, but he was none the less dear to me. I used to sit and write by the hour, and tell him about the wee funny house on the prairie and the stove out under a tree. We were baking bread in it one day when a storm came up and the cattle got scared and kicked over the stove, bread and all.

By September the wind would blow across the prairie, windy and cold. We knew that we must do something with our cabin to keep us warm. Mr. Strang had lots of experiences and escapades in New Zealand and Australia before we were married, so it comes good to know many things. He said we will sod up to the eves. I was always one with him to help, so he fell to and cut the squares of sod and I would build. While we worked we sang the song of David, especially the one that was our favorite and we could join in together. "I to the hills together will lift up my eyes." Sung to the time of French. It was mighty and how we should sing out, till Mrs. Beach who lived across the prairies could hear us.

We still held on to the way we were brought up. To sing a psalm and read a chapter. The house was a lot warmer after we laid the sod up to the eves, little knowing the many long winter days we had to spend inside that wee shanty. Everything in it was homemade. My husband was clever with a hammer and saw. Made chairs and tables and what we needed to get along with. Motherhood was coming on me pretty soon. I was busy indeed trying to fashion the little garments out of what I had. I was always glad I had so many good cloths so I could make what was needed.

We women would try to comfort each other and when I would get a letter from home it was like a sacred thing to me, and I would cry for several days and wish I could see them again and dream of my mother at night until I would have to be woke up. It got colder and colder. Forty below was quite common, then we could hear the coyotes howling at night and I would be so afraid. The first Christmas and New Years Day were very quiet. The Stewarts and us got together and had dinner the best that we could. On the first day of January our Robert was born, a fine healthy ten pounds. How proud we were of him. I used to take him on long walks when spring came. My brother, Andrew, used to send me a good sized check once in a while. It was such a comfort to us. Others of the colony kept coming out until there were ten families. We kept learning to plant seeds and hoe and plant tators and corn and our garden was right along side of the road. People passing would stop and wonder over the fragrance filled air.

There was the grandest rutabagas and tomatoes and onions. Everything did fine. Our teams were not heavy enough to do our own breaking till the following spring. We weren't afraid of work. We were early risers, up and doing the chores. The stock

grew and our cows multiplied. I made butter and sold it in town. We built another log house and barn by that time things began to look like we were going to have a farm worthwhile.

We always go to church in Wadena, walking through the slough. We had a rusty bridge across the creek. We built our second house down by the creek, and by this time we had three children. I must let you know how we spent the 4th of July. Mr. Langley sent word that he would come for us as the town folks wanted to see how many were on homesteads all around. So, they got up a banquet, but we made baskets of our own, then we came to great grief before we got there.

The county got flooded with so much rain. We had the oxen, and Stewarts joined with us. We got the children all be-curled and dressed in their best, and so did we all. We put plenty quilts in the wagon and started out. When we got to the creek it was up over the fields. We had to wade over the poles across the creek, the men carrying the children over first. The creek was rampant. Mrs. Stewart was telling me, if I didn't step square on the tufts of grass, I would go down into the water. She had just told me when down she went herself. Her clothes were all wet. That was why she was afraid to cross the creek, but we all got over it.

Then the men tackled the oxen, but they got caught by the horns of the second team and they had a hard time getting them out. The wagon went down the creek, wagon, lunches, quilts and all. The men went after it and got it up on the bank. While this was happening, I got Mrs. Stewart's things all dried out on the bushes and she got all fixed up again. Everything was ready again and we got started. We had another time getting through the big slough but we got out. It was nearly 4 p.m. before we got into Wadena. The banquet was over, our lunches were ruined, and we had never been so hungry in all of our lives. When they saw us coming they all crowded around us to hear our experiences of getting in for the 4th of July, and when they saw our lunches were wet, they were very nice to fix a table so we could get something to eat, which we did ample justice to, we were so hungry.

Mrs. Hurst was building the hotel and had the first floor done. They were going to have a dance and Jack Stewart came for me and Mr. Strang got Mrs. Stewart to dance a set of quadrilles. We were all in readiness when we heard the call "Set to your partners, give her a twist and all run away." We could not go through with it. We had never heard the like before but we had so much fun over it, before we got through. We danced a good Scotch roll and they all stood still to see us do the old home dances and then we put out for home because it was late. That gave us something to talk about for a long time and kept us in amusement going over the incidents of the day.

We liked to go to church but it was a long eight miles over there and through the slough. This day we were a wee bit late, so when we got to the slough Mr. Strang said to me, "Don't bother to take your shoes off. I will make a seat with my hands at my back and we'll hurry through and get in time." Well, we were getting along fine when he made a misstep and down we went and he dropped me in a deep hole, shoes and all! But, nothing daunted, I got out, took my shoes and stockings off, wrung out my clothes and went on, dangling my shoes around my neck till we got outside of Wadena. Then I sat down and put them on and went to church to hear a good sermon from Rev. Kerr.

We hurried home again, hungry as hawks. After while they fixed the roads so that it was only half the distance. Many a time I've walked to town, carrying my butter and eggs to my customers. I love to walk, and would get home in time to make a good supper for the children coming home from school. They only had a dry lunch at noon and were always ready to have a hearty supper. Then to get the cows home and Mr. Strang and the two boys would milk while I would do the dishes and pans to strain the milk into.

After the work was done, I would read a story to them or they would play some game and I would get the babies to bed. Pretty soon we would all be in the land of nod, then up early and into a good honest day of work. Perhaps a sick neighbor would need me to run in and see what I could do for them. We had no doctor near us, so we had to wait on each other and do the best we could.

We never let Christmas or New Years go by without a general invitation to meet in one of our homes and have a tree for the children and a good dinner for all, with jokes and yarn swapping. We had a general good time, not forgetting a good Scotch reel and other things. Jim Robb supplied the music. A piece of paper over a comb just did a fine job with a tune whistled through it. We would step out full of blithe and have a good time singing the old Scotch songs, telling stories and the Wilson family were quite an addition to the Scotch Colony, getting up some pieces from Seth Wilson Scott's Works and various other Scotts pieces. They were all pretty good singers and all had pretty good organs, which was a wonderful help until the wee hours when they would all get around and sing together. It was wonderful how they learned to sing and play by guess or by golly on many a long winter's night.

We worked hard, were up early and got a good days work done. Our teams were heavy enough now so my husband could be up by 4 a.m. and out breaking ground. He broke 30 acres during a summer, and did the grubbing also. Our boys were beginning to be quite a help, and then had to have a hired man to see to cutting the corn, taters, rutabagas, etc. We always had a good garden and my flowers were a sight to behold.

Then the hay came ready to cut. We bought 40 acres of hayland from a Mr. Beach across the creek. We had 10 or 12 cows and had to have lots of hay for the long winters. Even churning every two days, I could sell all the butter I made in Wadena. Mary Wilson was the teacher in the little log school over the creek, where all the children went from round about.

And I hope you were interested and find something interesting in the way we used to do things.

The William Smith family furnished this article about the family of Mrs. James (Margaret Arbucle) Strang. Mrs. Strang was 21 when she left Scotland. While living in Compton, Robert, Margaret, and Archie were born.

On August 30, 1891, they sold the farm to John Stewart, their neighbor, and moved to Oregon.

This piece was found in the COMPTON TOWNSHIP HISTORY, Otter Tail, MN.

Friendly Fire

It has been estimated that as many as 250,000 soldiers, or about 24 percent, of U.S. troops have been killed or wounded by fellow American soldiers in the 20th century. In 1943, in a battle on the Aleutian Islands, 35,000 Canadians and U.S. soldiers fought long hours only to find after the heavy fog lifted they had been shooting at each other! Stonewall Jackson lost his left arm, no thanks to rebel sharpshooters, who mistook him for a Union soldier. He died later from complications. In the case of General Lesley McNair, it was an especially sad mistake.

McNair hardly fitted the image of what a general should look like. Eisenhower, MacArthur, and Marshall were all over six feet tall. McNair had to stretch to make five-foot eight. He had blue eyes, a hook nose, and was called "Whitey," a name that originated among his friends in the small town of Verndale, Minnesota, where he was born. His fierce streak did not surface until after he graduated from West Point in 1904, eleventh in his class.

In the years that followed, Whitey McNair made quite a name for himself. At the end of World War I, he was the youngest general officer in the army.

According to the Army Historical Foundation, "During World War II, a number of U.S. Army generals achieved fame and glory on the battlefields of the European and Pacific Theaters. Generals Douglas MacArthur, George S. Patton, Omar N. Bradley, Mark Clark, and many others won great victories against the Germans and Japanese. These victories, however, would have been impossible without well-trained troops. The man largely responsible for the monumental task of building and training the Army during World War II, and, in effect, largely responsible for its successes, was Gen. Lesley J. McNair, the "brains of the Army" and commander of Army Ground Forces."

General McNair was credited with running a "tight ship." He was soft spoken, but hard boiled. He believed anyone who was born without leadership qualities should step aside, that anything in an office that was desirable but not necessary should be eliminated. He cut his staff to the bone and had no personal aide. He made his own hotel reservations and carried his bag. He was known to have any officer with a littered desk removed. He was especially feared by what he called "metallic generals," those with silver in their hair, gold in their teeth, and lead in their pants.

Those who worked closest with McNair knew little about his personal life. Not the name of his wife or how many children he had, he was so close mouthed. He had one son, also a West Pointer, and a wife. To relax he rode horseback every Sunday morning for three or four hours. He asked his wife to not accept any dinner invitations more than once a month from among the many dozens that came in.

In June 1944, McNair was posted to England to take command of the phantom 1st Army Group from Patton. While visiting the front again, he was killed by an errant American bomb during Operation Cobra near St. Lo, France, on July 25, 1944. He was the highest-ranking U.S. general killed in World War II.

Sod Shanty Home

I was born in Holstrop, Denmark, on May 22, 1842. I was baptized Marie Christensen. On the day of my confirmation I stood at the foot of my class. At the end stood a small white hired lad with big hands and feet. His name was Carl Johnson. I worked as a goose girl, nurse, and housekeeper until I was 28 years old when I met Charles again. He had just returned from America after working three years on a railroad. At a dance he asked me to go with him to America. My parents warned that he might sell me to a black man. I had no fear of that.

On April 13th, 1870, we and some of our friends left Copenhagen on the emigrant ship, "Ocean Queen" and at the end of nineteen days arrived in New York. To my sorrow, the chest holding all my special things had failed to be put on board this ship and would come at a later date. When? Peter Jorgensen's things were not there, either. Charles and the rest of the party would go on to Dakota Territory. I found work at Smith's emigrant home and at the end of three weeks the missing baggage arrived but we had to pay fifty dollars to get it. This was a calamity since we only had fifty-five dollars between us. However, the emigrant home allowed me to pack a large hamper of food for the trip to Dakota Territory. In the meantime Charles filed on a claim relinquished by a young homesteader. The claim was in Clay County, thirteen miles northwest of what is now Vermillion. Charles was at the Sioux City depot waiting for Charles and Mr. Jorgenson when I arrived. Roads were muddy and but a trail so they purchased two cows and tied them behind our wagon. From then on Charles and Mr. Jorgenson took turns walking the last twenty-five miles and prodding the cows. Neither dared to drive. At dusk at a small log cabin, a black dog named "June" ran out to help them and lick their hands. One night we had to stay at the home of an Indian family.

Next morning I took our inventory of my new home, one room, one window, one door, sod roof and floor. There was one kettle, one frying pan, a coffee pot. I also found two plates, two cups and saucers, two knives and forks. There was an old stove, a bed and table made of rough lumber and a bench.

Our first day was spent in walking to Rev. Christenson's homestead two miles south to be married. Here, also, was but one room and in order to not embarrass the young couple Rev. Christenson went outside to remove his coat while he put on his robe and collar. We walked back again as husband and wife and near our door stood the red cow named "Squaw," licking a new calf. "Our wedding gift," said Charles.

That first winter Charles spent a good deal of his time in falling trees that grew along the Missouri river. The logs were for a new house. We also needed fuel. One day while I was alone I heard June making an unusual lot of noise. I was just going to open the door when it was opened from outside. Here stood two young Indians, spattered with blood, holding hunting knives and a gun. I was frightened but I neither screamed or fainted. June stood at my side. One Indian handed me a paper from his pocket. I looked it over, nodded as if I understood. I could not read a word, nor could he. They then motioned for something to eat. I gave them bread and coffee. The Indians then wanted flour and salt which I also gave them, hoping they would leave which they did. Then one returned carrying the heart and liver of an antelope in his hands. These he deposited on the table. My fright vanished when I saw the reason for their blood spattered clothing. They had shot and dressed an antelope.

That same fall other guests were in the form of a flock of geese. On their way south they were stopping to feed in a nearby field where oat had been harvested. Charles was a good shot and had a good gun but not one bullet. This was a calamity. I had brought along a clock carefully wrapped in a feather tick but in spite of all the pains I had taken to keep it

in good condition it refused to tick tick in this new land. The pendulum had two heavy weights of lead. Of these he made bullets. When everything was ready Charles took a horse that he knew did not fear shooting and walked along side of it close to the geese. He pulled the trigger and when the smoke cleared there lay seven geese.

My next home was also log, much like the first but larger and it had a "lean to" for a bedroom. It also had board floor and shingle roof, a great improvement, now we did not have to sit on the bed under an umbrella in a rain. In this house ten of my eleven children were born. In 1878 just eight years after we located we build a large brick barn which still stands. All the brick were made and burned on

the farm. They were planning to build a brick house in the near future, then came the flood of 1881. However, the brick house was built in due time.

Of my eleven children, only eight lived to grow up. We all worked with the faith that "things" would get better, and they did. Charles was a good husband and father.

Post script: Marie Johnson lived to be ninety-eight years old. She never went back to her native Denmark. She said America had given her a good home and family and she never forgot how sick she was on the "Ocean Queen." Marie and Charles are buried in the Danish-Lutheran Cemetery south of Gayville, South Dakota one mile from their original homestead.

Information given by Mrs. Chris Sorenson, their daughter.

Nelson Wells, Homesteader

In 1902, neither fame or fortune smiled on Nelson Wells of rural Verndale, Minnesota. He had to chop both out of a soil with the properties of granite. After burying his first wife, mother of three of his children, Nelson left "Wildcat Corners" for Palo Alto Township, Iowa. In a few years, he headed back to a place known as "Cook's Corners," near Verndale, with a second wife and two daughters.

In 1908, Lady Luck tossed a smile Nelson's direction and he got the federal job of mail carrier on Route Four. His wife filled in as substitute carrier the few times he was unable to go, thus keeping the money in the family. Nelson had the route set up so that he met another carrier from Wing River Town Hall, took the mail home to sort it, then with a fresh horse went the 24 miles to Oylen, getting back home before dark. The next day he would use the same horse to go to the hall where he picked up the horse he had left there for a rest.

One of the stories assistant carrier Mrs. Wells tells goes like this: "One snowy morning, my husband's back went out. He couldn't move or take a deep breath, he was in bed and unable to go with the mail. I realized that I had to make the 30 mile drive and delivery route, so I sent the hired man to get a neighbor girl to come and stay with my children and look after my sick husband. I started out with the faithful old horse hitched to the mail cab to do my regular duty as a substitute mail carrier. Much of the 30 mile route was through the pine woods, with houses far a part, and some of them a long ways from their mail box. The snow was deep already and much of the track. No one else seemed to be out, and how white the snow looked!

"After a while the snow began coming down in earnest. The weather was not extremely cold yet, for which I was thankful and the wind was stilled. The flakes came so thick and fast it began to seem almost like a thick blanket pressing down, trying to cover me. Seem's like I never saw snow come so fast. The horse found it hard going and became leg weary

Nelson Wells - Homesteader

breaking track, but still plodded on.

"Thirty miles for that old horse to go before the short winter day was over! My thoughts ran on and on, how were the folks at home doing? Would old Dan really get me back home? I had plenty of time to worry. Late in the afternoon, when I stopped at one of the mail boxes, my horse went down in the snow. I tried to get him up, got out and waded around in the deep some and worked to get him up, when I finally succeeded I found that one shaft was broken. No one to call. No house near. No telephone anywhere. What could I do? It had turned bitterly cold.

"I knew of a log cabin farther on and started for that. The family heard my problem, but would not consent to take me farther than the next neighbor, which was about three miles away. They said they would take his team and sled and myself and the rest of the mail route. Mrs. Lee insisted on getting me something to eat while Mr. Lee finished up his chores and made plans to be away the rest of the day. Imagine

my worries about the home folks! I knew they would be worried about me, not knowing where or why I had been detained so late.

"Well, the road seemed long, but I finally reached my home about 11 p.m., but in the meantime, the hired man had started out on horseback on orders from my husband, to look for me. In the darkness he missed the road and wandered around in the woods, lost for a long time. I got home

before he did. So, ended a long work day with the mail on a short winter day."

Nelson ran this mail route until 1919, being forced to retire because he reached the age of 65. His work as mail carrier was beyond reproach; the predominating part of his service was his outstanding honesty. He was a good provider and left behind well cared for land on the Wing River, where he resided for 20 years.

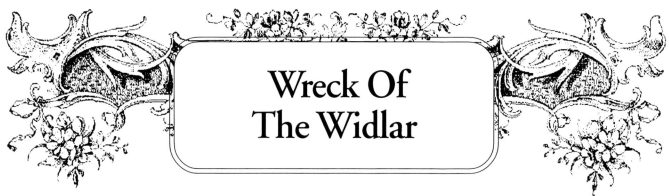

Wreck Of
The Widlar

When Captain Forbes took the Frances Widlar out of Duluth in November 1920, carrying ore he had no thought that in 24 hours his ship would be breaking up. Caught in a snow storm, the ship rammed into Pancake Shoals near Whitefish Bay. She could not fight against a pounding sea and was breaking up under their feet. A call to Coast Guard station Crisp Point went unanswered. A scared stiff crew tried to find a bit of shelter as ice grew on their ship. They could feel it breaking up beneath them.

Sixty-three hours later, misery had increased and three men felt they had to make a dangerous move to save the rest. Lashing themselves together they slowly edged their way to the galley where there was food. While frigid waves broke over the ship they passed out soaked crackers. As darkness closed down for night fog drifted in on the miserable crew. Forbes knew his crew would be dead by morning unless something was done. He ordered the six strongest sailors to try to launch a boat and pull for the nearest shore. The rest cried as fog and waves swallowed the little boat. It was snowing harder and the temperature had dropped.

The six in the boat bent to their task. They were wondering how many more strokes they could pull when a dark shape loomed right in front of them. It was the steamer Livingston who took them aboard. A distress call was sent out to Soo for help as well as Iowa, a giant tug. That tug along with a little fishing boat made three trips getting the stranded crew ashore. The entire crew was rescued as well as the one that was most unusual baggage. Captain Forbes had taken his daughter's little dog "Toostie." The little rascal's antics all those hours had been great for the trapped crew's morale, claiming their attentions away from those greedy gray waves.

Widlar was towed back to dry dock and salvaged. She was fitted to go back to work on the lakes. Captain Forbes was not her captain when she went back in July of 1966. Forbes went west where he passed credits to be captain of a salt water command. Following that he finally realized a dream when he became skipper of his own fleet of tuna boats. He died in 1946, having spent his entire adult life on one big piece of water or another.

The Crewmembers That Day
List of Crewmembers of the Francis Widlar on that November day in 1920 donated by Emerald (Peggy) Forbe Baker:

Captain: Arthur FORBES, Ashtabula, Ohio

Second Mate: K. CAHOURS, St. Clair, Michigan

Deck Hand: Alex MCDONALD, Detroit, Michigan

Chief Engineer: Tom SHERIDAN, Cleveland, Ohio

First Mate: Gus LAMBERT, New Orleans, Louisiana

Boatswain: H. J. BONNAK, Algonac, Michigan

Wheelsman: Harry AYRES, Ashtabula, Ohio

Wheelsman: E. R. MERMUYS, Two River, Wisconsin

Watchman: Jim BILEDEAU, Superior, Wisconsin

Watchman: John G. MORGAN, Chicago, Illinois

Deckhand: Dennis WALLACE, Lorain, Ohio

Deckhand: J. QUINN, New York City, New York

Deckhand: Frank HRICKIERVIEZ, Cicero, Illinois
R, St. Mary's, Pennsylvania

Third Engineer: B. D. DIEDRICH, Lorain, Ohio

Oiler: George PETRICK, Cleveland, Ohio

Oiler: A. F. SCHLEMEN, St. Mary's, Pennsylvania

Clara Seager, Cook

It was 1879 when Clara Seager stepped off the train into a cloud of dust. She looked up and down a rutted street with surprise. So many tents, buildings halfway finished, teams hauling heavy loads of lumber. So this was what a frontier town looked like! Clara was a widow with one daughter, Isobell. They stood a minute, then after getting their land legs headed for what a faded sign declared to be "The Headquarters Hotel." After getting something to eat and finding a place for them to spend the night, Clara needed a job. It so happened that George Swartz was asking the manager where he might hire a cook when Clara and Isobell walked past. Almost in mid-step she turned toward him. "Sir, I really need to work and I can cook. There would be two of us. My daughter stays with me." George took inventory at a glance, saying, "You just got a job, Ma'm. Meet me here in an hour. We have a bit of a ride to the ranch."

The "bit of a ride" was more than twenty miles west of Fargo over a road so rough all four wheels were seldom on the ground the same time. Her job was to feed a harvest crew three big square a day with lunches in between. In a month, when George told her the harvest was finished and he no longer had need for a cook, Clara was delighted. She had never worked any harder than she had the last month. It had been good of him to take no notice of Isobell, like she wasn't there. Some would have docked her pay. On the ride back into Fargo, he said, "Attorney Lowell's wife died a coupla weeks ago. He's havin' a time with his kids. I'll let you off in front of his office."

Attorney Jacob Lowell was sitting in a leather chair, dwarfed by a huge desk. He hadn't listened to more than half of Clara's spiel before interrupting her, to say, "I live a mile north on this road. The doors open and there'll be a brat or two around. You can have the little room off the kitchen."

Clara dived into a job that left her spent by night. Again, she was thankful he hadn't mentioned Isobell. She had never seen a pack of wilder younguns and in the spring when Attorney Lowell announced his engagement to a healthy country girl Clara packed with joy.

The next cooking job was for the Armenia Sharon Land Company, a bonanza farm of 30,000 acres with a crew of 30 men. The meals were planned and Clara had never worked so hard. Keeping this bunch in pie at least twice a week; baking bread every day. Thank goodness she had a flunky who came on wash day. The men's clothes were put in a barrel of hot suds and beat with a stomper. The Chaffee family who owned the ranch came from Connecticut and were very religious. Their only son, Bert, went down with the Titanic. Eben Chaffee ran a tight ship.

Clara met John Dulow on the farm. He was a field hand. It was on one of their evening walks that they became engaged. They were married in December 1880 by a Methodist preacher and went to live on John's humble homestead. Humble or not, having at last a home of her own was wonderful to Clara. She didn't seem to mind the rough walls made of thick livery lumber, or the raw two-by-fours. Paper covered the outside, held down with lathe strips. It was unfurnished and so drafty the wind came through the cracks and blew the lamp out.

The next years went fast for Clara. John was a good worker and little by little they built a better house and the shanty they had been living in became the barn. There was a war, making what they had to sell a decent price. Two boys and another girl came to them and were welcome. To get a herd of milk cows they saved all of the heifers for cows. A bad setback came one day that wiped them out.

Far off they heard a roaring noise. Before they could close the windows it was upon them. Hail

stones as big as eggs smashed windows, killed 100 of Clara's chickens, and raised large welts on the backs of the horses and cows. They made holes in the roof and flattened the crops. Never had things been harder, they thought. Then trouble really came to roost at their house.

Clara had turned into a fairly good pioneer nurse, like a doctor some said. When there was trouble, she went. Then came the call to a home where a son had a high temperature and sore throat. Of course, Clara went. She took diphtheria germs home despite how careful she was. John was first to go, then the boys. For some reason men and boys got hit more often and harder than women and girls.

Left alone again, with two daughters instead of one, Clara sold the farm to a neighbor who wanted more land. She had enough money to send the girls to boarding school or teacher school. Attorney Lowell's second wife died the year before and his family were also at boarding schools. Clara spent the last useful years of her life doing light cooking for herself and the attorney, almost back to where she had started.

Drop-Off Days In Dawson

In 1870, up to a half-million head of long horns were dropped off in Dawson, North Dakota. It was halfway to Evarts, the end of the line, when both cattle and men sorely needed a break from each other. After Evarts, came the long harrowing trek to Velva, North Dakota, where they boarded a train again on the last leg of their journey to Canada. In Canada, lush green pastures awaited, where grass grew knee high. A few months of that on the menu and cattle made the return trip sleek and fat.

The Sibley Hotel in Dawson was a favorite of drivers. It had sleeping rooms upstairs with a saloon below. The story goes that one cowboy tired to the bone from a long drive was too disturbed by the hullabaloo from below to sleep decided to quiet them. He bucked his gun on over the "Long Johns" he was sleeping in, madder 'n a wet hen. On his way down stairs he shot two large plate glass mirrors off the wall. Some puncher saw him coming and shot the gun out of his hand. As it hit the gun it broke his wrist.

It was discovered later that when he got out of bed a shot from some drunken bum below had come through the floor, entering his heel and going part way up his leg.

What a price to pay for a little quiet!

The Brooklyn Bay Bridge Story

Take pneumatic caissons and excavate a spot on the East River. Now lay a foundation for a pier by using air pressure to pump out the sand, then a clamshell dredge. While you are doing this the caisson will slowly be sinking until it settles on solid bedrock. There. You just followed the directions, as drawn by bridge builder John Roebling, for the foundation of the famous Brooklyn Bay Bridge. His son, Washington Roebling, laid the foundation, but Washington's wife, Emily Warren Roebling, built the bridge.

John Roebling died with lock jaw after stepping on a splinter in 1869 two weeks before the work was to start. After overseeing most of the foundation built, Washington became a pitiful invalid, partially paralyzed and confined to bed with decompression disease or "the bends." That is when Emily took over.

Emily Roebling was no run-of-the-mill 1862 housewife. From the first scratch on paper she had been vitally interested and caught up in the project. She knew the bridge was to be 1,500 feet longer than any other suspension bridge in existence. A commodity filled with potential but as yet short on being tried was the wire rope invented by John Roebling and manufactured on his farm. Commonly used hemp rope was bulky, unmanageable when wet, and rotted. A cable made of 286 wires was only an inch and one-fourth in diameter.

The education Emily enjoyed was most unusual for a girl in 1862. Emily was from a family of builders, the "Warrens," who encouraged her interest in mathematics. She was taught higher mathematics, the calculation of catenary curves, strength of materials, stress analysis, bridge specifications and cable construction. Even so, this impressive amount of knowledge in what was strictly a man's field of endeavour in 1869 did not stop a board of inquiry from rightfully worrying about the bridge. Using the wire cable cost more than rope and the price went up. Would Washington be able to ever take command again? Emily so earnestly entreated them to give her a chance with her husband's direction, they decided

John A. Roebling

Emily Roebling

to do that. This would not have worked if Washington had not shared every bit of knowledge, every plan, every scrap with her. He held back nothing. Hers was so retentive a mind, a mathematician with the yen to learn, that between them they succeeded. He was bed-ridden for years, becoming less and less involved while she gradually took over. It took 14 long years to build the bridge.

The big bridge was half built when trustees decided they needed to know exactly how things were progressing. Washington had grown less interested and weaker. Politics had reared its ugly head and there were battles of descent that could stop construction even at this late date, removing an obviously ill man from the head job.

What seemed at the outset to be a catastrophe to Emily was actually a blessing. It provided the exposure she needed to prove that she was knowledgeable and efficient. Her talk to the prestigious American Society of Civil Engineers was the first time a woman had formally been asked to address this association. It rocketed her into a position where she was noticed. In fact, she was hard to miss as she clamored over construction in long skirts.

The Brooklyn Bay Bridge opened on May 24, 1883, while bands played, parades and politicians waved and marched, gala dinners were held, and what was claimed to be 14 tons of fireworks split

the sky. In a speech President Chester A. Arthur called it "The Eighth Wonder Of The World." Newspapers reported that Emily Roebling was "beautiful and vivacious." Washington Roebling, a hero of the Civil War and still official chief engineer of the Brooklyn Bridge, was unmoved and pale. He could stand no longer than ten minutes.

When it came to giving credit Emily's name was not left out. A plaque for her hangs on one of the towers; one for her husband and father-in-law on the other. Emily Warren was the youngest child in a family of 17 children. She was wife, mother, lecturer, student, bridge builder, world traveler, and club woman. Emily graduated from law school at New York University when she was 55. Even so, some men still find it hard to acknowledge her. There are books written around the bridge that scarcely mention her.

Emily was instrumental in "breaking-the-ice" for women going into the technical field. Few women of that time were credited with so much honor by men. She was voted vice-president of the Daughters of the American Revolution, was active in women's suffrage and a member of the Huguenot Society.

One of fates unlikely but true twists, after all the hoopla from the Brooklyn Bay Bridge was over, was when Washington Roebling regained his health to outlive Emily by 20 years.

In fact, he got married again!

Amazon Mary

Amazon Mary Fields was over six feet tall, weighed more than 225 pounds, and was never without at least one gun. Mary was born about 1832, as a slave. She grew up an orphan, never married or had children. The nuns in a convent were her family; the players on the local baseball team were her brothers. Judge Fields owned Mary so she took his last name.

One of Mary's first jobs after the Civil War that gave her freedom was working as a chambermaid aboard the Robert E. Lee Steamboat. She was along on the famous race to Natchez in 1870. The sailors on board were rougher and tougher than on any other craft on the Mississippi. Mary smoked cigars, learned to cuss, knock a man out with one blow, drink, shoot and play poker. She gave up the job but kept her bad habits when she went to work at St. Peter's Convent in Cascade, Montana. Her work was either riding or driving wild horses, something she could do as well as any man, so she also dressed like one.

On one of the trips Mary made, she was returning visitors to the stage and was on her way back. It was far into the night and the howls of huge timber wolves came from all quarters. They were moving in. Red eyes showed in every direction.

The horses were in a panic, took the bits in their teeth, and lunged down the trail. The harness broke sending the cart to overturn in the ditch. Her load of supplies were dumped everywhere. Pulling one of her guns Mary picked a spot halfway between glowing red eyes and pulled the trigger until it began to get light in the east and they faded back into the timber. Eight huge wolves lay dead. Soon a r ig came from the convent to rescue her and the supplies. Mary quit that job in 1887.

But getting another job Amazon Mary took time off to renew friendships, visit old haunts, and enjoy herself. She played poker with the best of them, had a gun duel (and won!) with one umbrae, and knocked out everyone she fought with. She was credited with breaking more noses than anyone else in history. Finally, she needed money and had to have a job. Carrying the mail was a tough and demanding one that soon wore out both men and their animals. Mary was only the second woman in history to manage a route and wild, half-broken horses. She became "Stagecoach Mary". She did this for eight years, until she was injured by a horse out of control.

Mary's next move was to start a laundering business doing clothes for miners and cowboys. Whenever she wasn't scrubbing dirty clothes she was perched on a bar stool drinking anything in a glass. She waited to shoot one man who didn't pay a $2 laundry bill until he was cleaning out a latrine. After she shot him, she just rolled him in. Amazon Mary was heavy and powerful. She had taken to carrying a pair of six-shooters and a shotgun. She like to fight.

Aside from all of this. Mary showed a soft side before she died of liver problems when she was eighty. She made boutonnieres for all of the members of the Cascade baseball team when they won a game. On the day she was buried there was no school because she knew and loved all of the children. Saloons locked their door during her funeral so they all could go. Some of Amazon Mary's most happy times, other than when she decked somebody, was watching over the small charges that she baby sat. Famous cowboy artist Charlie Russell and actor Gary Cooper were among them.

When Amazon Mary knew her days or even hours were numbered, she took a couple of blankets and sneaked away into the brush and high weeds behind her two room cabin to lie down and die. She did not want to make trouble for anyone. Children found her and she was taken to Columbus Hospital in Great Falls. There was no lack of sitters, since everyone wanted to be with her.

Amazon Mary Fields lies at rest now in a small cemetery along side the road between Cascade and St. Peter's Mission, the road she had traveled so many years.

Wrong Restless Corpse

The death of Columbus did not put an end to his challenging the briny deep another few times. Columbus breathed his last on May 20th, 1506, in Valladolid, Spain. He was 54 years old and had been ailing for years, hastened by the death of his staunch supporter Queen Isabella. He died a depressed and disappointed man with not one thing he could point to that, as far as he knew, turned out to be successful. He saw his life as wasted.

Columbus was buried for a time in a small cemetery in Valladolid. After a period his body was reinterred in Seville, Spain. Twenty years later his oldest son, Diego, was also buried there. However, Diego's wife was not satisfied with the arrangement as she thought they deserved a more prestigious burial and petitioned the court to have both bodies moved to a Cathedral in Santo Domingo in Hispanola. This involved crossing the Atlantic where they were laid to rest beneath the right side of the altar.

Two centuries went by and it seemed that Columbus' travels were truly over. Not so, since France won the Hispanola Island from Spain in 1795. During these years Admiral Columbus' remains were regarded a national treasure; the remains were exhumed and taken to Havana, Cuba.

Another century passed during which Cuba achieved independence from Spain. The change made it necessary for Columbus to make one more long trip across the angry Atlantic Ocean back to Seville. In 1877 repairmen were restoring the Santo Domingo Cathedral. While digging under the left side of the altar they found a stout box with the name "Columbus" stenciled on it. It held human remains.

It was then that someone reasoned that the "left" and the "right" of the altar depended upon which side one faced it. That being true, it is more than merely possible, in fact, almost probable that it was not Columbus who crossed the mighty Atlantic two more times. The remains of Columbus likely never left Santo Domingo. Also, part of the remains in Seville were generously given to Genoa in 1872 for the Guadicentennial Celebration.

So actually, Columbus, where art thou?

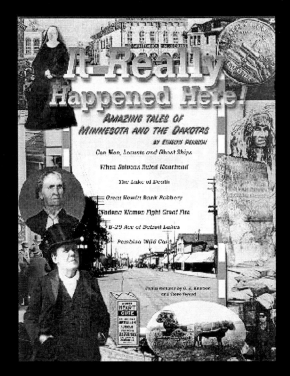

Book 1
It Really Happened Here!

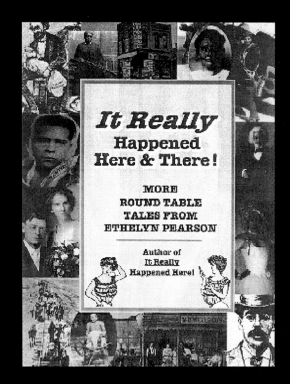

Book 2
It Really Happened Here & There!

PLEASE COMPLETE THE FOLLOWING TO ORDER ADDITIONAL COPIES

Please send me _____ It Really Happened Here! at **$24.95 each** *(plus $3.50 shipping & handling)*
Please send me _____ It Really Happened Here & There! at **$24.95 each** *(plus $3.50 shipping & handling)*

SEND THIS ORDER FORM TO:
McCleery & Sons Publishing
PO Box 248
Gwinner, ND 58040-0248

I am enclosing $_____
❏ Check ❏ Money Order

Payable in US funds. No cash accepted.

SHIP TO:
Name_____
Mailing Address _____
City _____
State/Zip _____

For credit card orders call 1-888-568-6329

Bill my: ❏ VISA ❏ MasterCard   Expires _____

Card # _____

Signature_____

Daytime Phone Number _____

OR Order On-Line at
www.jmcompanies.com

Shipping and Handling costs for larger quantites available upon request.

Orders by check allow longer delivery time.

Money order and credit card orders will be shipped within 48 hours.

This offer is subject to change without notice.

NEW RELEASES

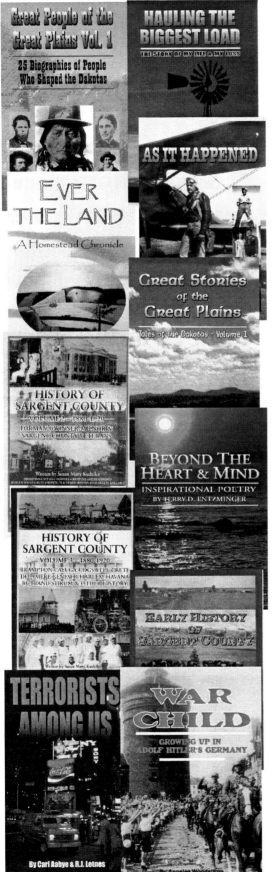

Great People of the Great Plains Vol. 1 *25 Biographies of People Who Shaped the Dakotas* This is the second book for Keith Norman and the first in this series. Keith has always had an interest in the history of the region. His radio show 'Great Stories of the Great Plains' is heard on great radio stations all across both Dakotas. While the biographies within this book are a bit too long to fit the time constraints of a radio show, listeners will find the events and people portrayed familiar. For more information on the radio show and a list of his current affiliates check out Norman's website at www.tumbleweednetwork.com. Written by Keith Norman - Author of *Great Stories of the Great Plains - Tales of the Dakotas* (124 pgs.) $14.95 each in a 6x9" paperback.

Ever The Land *A Homestead Chronicle-* This historical chronicle (non-fiction) traces the life of young Pehr through his youth in the 1800's, marriage, parenthood and tenant farming in Sweden; then his emigration to America and homesteading in Minnesota. Multifarious simple joys and woes, and one deep constant sorrow accompany Pehr to his grave in 1914. Written by: The late Ruben L. Parson (336 pgs.) $16.96 each in a 6x9" paperback.

History of Sargent County - Volume 2 - 1880-1920 *(Forman, Gwinner, Milnor & Sargent County Veterans)* Over 220 photos and seven chapters containing: Forman, Gwinner and Milnor, North Dakota history with surveyed maps from 1909. Plus Early History of Sargent County, World War I Veterans, Civil War Veterans and Sargent County Fair History. Written by: Susan Mary Kudelka - Author of *Early History of Sargent County - Volume 1* (224 pgs.) $16.95 each in a 6x9" paperback.

History of Sargent County - Volume 3 - 1880-1920 *(Brampton, Cayuga, Cogswell, Crete, DeLamere, Geneseo, Harlem, Havana, Rutland, Stirum & Other History)* - Over 280 photos and fifteen chapters containing: Brampton, Cayuga, Cogswell, Crete, DeLamere, Geneseo, Harlem, Havana, Rutland and Stirum, North Dakota histories with surveyed maps from 1909. Plus history on Sargent County in WWI, Sargent County Newspapers, E. Hamilton Lee and bonus photo section. Written by: Susan Mary Kudelka - Author of *Early History of Sargent County - Volume 1* (220 pgs.) $16.95 each in a 6x9" paperback.

Terrorists Among Us - This piece of fiction was written to "expose a weakness" in present policies and conflicts in the masses of rules which seem to put emphasis on business, money, and power interests at the expense of the people's security, safety and happiness. Shouldn't we and our leaders strive for some security for our people? Written by Carl Aabye & R.J. Letnes. (178 pgs.) $15.95 each in a 6x9" paperback.

Hauling the Biggest Load - *The Story of My Life & My Loss* - This is an unusual story because of the many changes that have happened since the author's birth in 1926. In May 2002, he lost his son, John, in a car accident. None of those other experiences seemed important anymore... Richard needed something to try and take his mind off that tragedy. "I thought I had hauled some big loads in my life but I never had to have a load as big as this one." Written by: Richard Hamann (144 pages) $14.95 each in 6x9" paperback.

As It Happened - Over 40 photos and several chapters containing Allen Saunders' early years, tales of riding the rails, his Navy career, marriage, Army instruction, flying over "The Hump", and his return back to North Dakota. Written by Allen E. Saunders. (74 pgs) $12.95 each in a 6x9" paperback.

Great Stories of the Great Plains - *Tales of the Dakotas - Vol. 1* - The radio show "Great Stories of the Great Plains" is heard on great radio stations all across both Dakotas. Norman has taken some of the stories from broadcasts, added some details, and even added some complete new tales to bring together this book of North and South Dakota history. Written by Keith Norman. (134 pgs.) $14.95 each in a 6x9" paperback.

Beyond the Heart & Mind *Inspirational Poetry by Terry D. Entzminger* - Beyond the Heart & Mind is the first in a series of inspirational poetry collections of Entzminger. Read and cherish over 100 original poems and true-to-the-heart verses printed in full color in the following sections: Words of Encouragement, On the Wings of Prayer, God Made You Very Special, Feelings From Within, The True Meaning of Love, and Daily Joys. (120 pgs.) $12.95 each in a 6x9" paperback.

Early History of Sargent County - *Volume 1* - Over seventy photos and thirty-five chapters containing the early history of Sargent County, North Dakota: Glacial Movement in Sargent County, Native Americans in Sargent County, Weather, Memories of the Summer of 1883, Fight for the County Seat, Townships, Surveyed Maps from 1882 and much more. Written by Susan M. Kudelka. (270 pgs.) $16.95 each in a 6x9" paperback.

War Child - *Growing Up in Adolf Hitler's Germany* - Annelee Woodstrom was 20 years old when she immigrated to America in 1947. These kind people in America wanted to hear about Adolf Hitler. During her adolescence, constant propaganda and strictly enforced censorship influenced her thinking. As a young adult, the bombings and all the consequential suffering caused by World War II affected Annelee deeply. How could Annelee tell them that as a child, during 1935, she wanted nothing more than to be a member of Adolf Hitler's Jung Maidens' organization? Written by Annelee Woodstrom (252 pgs.) $16.95 each in a 6x9" paperback.

THE HASTINGS SERIES

Blue Darkness *(First in a Series of Hastings Books)* - This tale of warm relationships and chilling murders takes place in the lake country of central Minnesota. Normal activities in the small town of New Dresden are disrupted when local resident, ex-CIA agent Maynard Cushing, is murdered. His killer, Robert Ranforth also an ex-CIA agent, had been living anonymously in the community for several years. to the anonymous ex-agent. Stalked and attached at his country home, he employs tools and people to mount a defense and help solve crimes. Written by Ernest Francis Schanilec (author of The Towers). (276 pgs.) $16.95 each in a 6x9" paperback.

The Towers *(Second in a Series of Hastings Books)* - Tom Hastings has moved from the lake country of central Minnesota to Minneapolis. His move was precipitated by the trauma associated with the murder of one of his neighbors. After renting an apartment on the 20th floor of a high-rise apartment building known as The Towers, he's met new friends and retained his relationship with a close friend, Julie, from St. Paul. Hastings is a resident of the high-rise for less than a year when a young lady is found murdered next to a railroad track, a couple of blocks from The Towers. The murderer shares the same elevators, lower-level garage and other areas in the high-rise as does Hastings. The building manager and other residents, along with Hastings are caught up in dramatic events that build to a crisis while the local police are baffled. Who is the killer? Written by Ernest Francis Schanilec. (268 pgs.) $16.95 each in a 6x9" paperback.

Danger In The Keys *(Third in a Series of Hastings Books)* - Tom Hastings is looking forward to a month's vacation in Florida. While driving through Tennessee, he witnesses an automobile leaving the road and plunging down a steep slope. He stops and assists another man in finding the car. The driver, a young woman, survives the accident. Tom is totally unaware that the young woman was being chased because she had chanced coming into possession of a valuable gem, which had been heisted from a Saudi Arabian prince in a New York hotel room. After arriving in Key Marie Island in Florida, Tom checks in and begins enjoying the surf and the beach. He meets many interesting people, however, some of them are on the island because of the Guni gem, and they will stop at nothing in order to gain possession. Desperate people and their greedy ambitions interrupt Tom's goal of a peaceful vacation.
Written by Ernest Francis Schanilec (210 pgs.)
$16.95 each in a 6x9" paperback.

Purgatory Curve *(Fourth in a Series of Hastings Books)* - A loud horn penetrated the silence on a September morning in New Dresden, Minnesota. Tom Hastings stepped onto the Main Street sidewalk after emerging from the corner Hardware Store. He heard a freight train coming and watched in horror as it crushed a pickup truck that was stalled on the railroad tracks. Moments before the crash, he saw someone jump from the cab. An elderly farmer's body was later recovered from the mangled vehicle. Tom was interviewed by the sheriff the next day and was upset that his story about what he saw wasn't believed. The tragic death of the farmer was surrounded with controversy and mysterious people, including a nephew who taunted Tom after the accident. Or, was it an accident? Written by Ernest Francis Schanilec (210 pgs.) $16.95 each in a 6x9" paperback.

• •

March on the Dakota's - *The Sibley Expedition of 1863* - Following the military action of 1862, the U. S. government began collecting an army at various posts and temporary stockades of the state, in preparation for a move northwestward to the Dakota Territories in the early summer of 1863. The campaign was organized by General John Pope, with the intent to subdue the Sioux. Two expeditions were planned, one under General H. H. Sibley, organized in Minnesota, and the other under the Command of General Alfred Sully. Interesting facts, actual accounts taken from soldiers' journals, campsite listings, casualties and record of troops also included. Written by Susan Mary Kudelka. (134pgs.) $14.95 each in a 6x9" paperback.

The SOE on Enemy Soil - *Churchill's Elite Force* - British Prime Minister Winston Churchill's plan for liberating Europe from the Nazis during the darkest days of the Second World War was ambitious: provide a few men and women, most of them barely out of their teens, with training in subversion and hand-to-hand combat, load them down with the latest in sophisticated explosives, drop them by parachute into the occupied countries, then sit back and wait for them to "Set Europe Ablaze." No story has been told with more honesty and humor than Sergeant Fallick tells his tale of service. The training, the fear, the tragic failures, the clandestine romances, and the soldiers' high jinks are all here, warmly told from the point of view of "one bloke" who experienced it all and lived to tell about it. Written by R.A. Fallick. (282 pgs.) $16.95 each in a6x9" paperback.

Grandmother Alice - *Memoirs from the Home Front Before Civil War into 1930's* - Alice Crain Hawkins could be called the 'Grandma Moses of Literature'. Her stories, published for the first time, were written while an invalid during the last years of her life. These journal entries from the late 1920's and early 30's give us a fresh, novel and unique understanding of the lives of those who lived in the upper part of South Carolina during the state's growing years. Alice and her ancestors experiences are filled with understanding - they are provacative and profound. Written by Reese Hawkins (178 pgs.) $16.95 each in a 6x9" paperback.

Tales & Memories of Western North Dakota - *Prairie Tales & True Stories of 20th Century Rural Life*
This manuscript has been inspired with Steve's antidotes, bits of wisdom and jokes (sometimes ethnic, to reflect the melting pot that was and is North Dakota; and from most unknown sources). A story about how to live life with humor, courage and grace along with personal hardships, tragedies and triumphs. Written by Steve Taylor. (174 pgs.) $14.95 each in a 6x9" paperback.

Phil Lempert's HEALTHY, WEALTHY, & WISE - *The Shoppers Guide for Today's Supermarket*
This is the must-have tool for getting the most for your money in every aisle. With this valuable advice you will never see (or shop) the supermarket the same way again. You will learn how to: save at least $1,000 a year on your groceries, guarantee satisfaction on every shopping trip, get the most out of coupons or rebates, avoid marketing gimmicks, create the ultimate shopping list, read and understand the new food labels, choose the best supermarkets for you and your family. Written by Phil Lempert. (198 pgs.) $9.95 each in a 6x9" paperback.

Miracles of COURAGE - *The Larry W. Marsh Story* - This story is for anyone looking for simple formulas for overcoming insurmountable obstacles. At age 18, Larry lost both legs in a traffic accident and learned to walk again on untested prosthesis. No obstacle was too big for him - putting himself through college - to teaching a group of children that frustrated the whole educational system - to developing a nationally recognized educational program to help these children succeed. Written by Linda Marsh. (134 pgs.)$12.95 each in a 6x9" paperback.

The Garlic Cure - Learn about natural breakthroughs to outwit: Allergies, Arthritis, Cancer, Candida Albicans, Colds, Flu and Sore Throat, Environmental and Body Toxins, Fatigue, High Cholesterol, High Blood Pressure and Homocysteine and Sinus Headaches. The most comprehensive, factual and brightly written health book on garlic of all times. INCLUDES: 139 GOURMET GARLIC RECIPES! Written by James F. Scheer, Lynn Allison and Charlie Fox. (240 pgs.)
$14.95 each in a 6x9" paperback.

I Took The Easy Way Out - *Life Lessons on Hidden Handicaps* - Twenty-five years ago, Tom Day was managing a growing business - holding his own on the golf course and tennis court. He was living in the fast lane. For the past 25 years, Tom has spent his days in a wheelchair with a spinal cord injury. Attendants serve his every need. What happened to Tom? We get an honest account of the choices Tom made in his life. It's a courageous story of reckoning, redemption and peace. Written by Thomas J. Day. (200 pgs.) $19.95 each in a 6x9" paperback.

9/11 and Meditation - *America's Handbook* - All Americans have been deeply affected by the terrorist events of and following 9-11-01 in our country. David Thorson submits that meditation is a potentially powerful intervention to ameliorate the frightening effects of such divisive and devastating acts of terror. This book features a lifetime of harrowing life events amidst intense pychological and social polarization, calamity and chaos; overcome in part by practicing the age-old art of meditation. Written by David Thorson. (110 pgs.)
$9.95 each in a 4-1/8 x 7-1/4" paperback.

From Graystone to Tombstone - *Memories of My Father Engolf Snortland 1908-1976* This haunting memoir will keep you riveted with true accounts of a brutal penitentiary to a manhunt in the unlikely little town of Tolna, North Dakota. At the same time the reader will emerge from the book with a towering respect for the author, a man who endured pain, grief and needless guilt -- but who learned the art of forgiving and writes in the spirit of hope. Written by Roger Snortland. (178 pgs.)
$16.95 each in a 6x9" paperback.

Blessed Are The Peacemakers *Civil War in the Ozarks* - A rousing tale that traces the heroic Rit Gatlin from his enlistment in the Confederate Army in Little Rock to his tragic loss of a leg in a Kentucky battle, to his return in the Ozarks. He becomes engaged in guerilla warfare with raiders who follow no flag but their own. Rit finds himself involved with a Cherokee warrior, slaves and romance in a land ravaged by war. Written by Joe W. Smith (444 pgs.)
$19.95 each in a 6 x 9 paperback

Pycnogenol® - Pycnogenol® for Superior Health presents exciting new evidence about nature's most powerful antioxidant. Pycnogenol® improves your total health, reduces risk of many diseases, safeguards your arteries, veins and entire circulation system. It protects your skin - giving it a healthier, smoother younger glow. Pycnogenol® also boosts your immune system. Read about it's many other beneficial effects. Written by Richard A. Passwater, Ph.D. (122 pgs.)
$5.95 each in a 4-1/8 x 6-7/8" paperback.

Remembering Louis L'Amour - Reese Hawkins was a close friend of Louis L'Amour, one of the fastest selling writers of all time. Now Hawkins shares this friendship with L'Amour's legion of fans. Sit with Reese in L'Amour's study where characters were born and stories came to life. Travel with Louis and Reese in the 16 photo pages in this memoir. Learn about L'Amour's lifelong quest for knowledge and his philosophy of life. Written by Reese Hawkins and his daughter Meredith Hawkins Wallin. (178 pgs.)
$16.95 each in a 5-1/2x8" paperback.

For Your Love - Janelle, a spoiled socialite, has beauty and breeding to attract any mate she desires. She falls for Jared, an accomplished man who has had many lovers, but no real love. Their hesitant romance follows Jared and Janelle across the ocean to exciting and wild locations. Join in a romance and adventure set in the mid-1800's in America's grand and proud Southland. Written by Gunta Stegura. (358 pgs.)
$16.95 each in a 6x9" paperback.

Bonanza Belle - In 1908, Carrie Amundson left her home to become employed on a bonanza farm. Carrie married and moved to town. One tragedy after the other befell her and altered her life considerably and she found herself back on the farm where her family lived the toiled during the Great Depression. Carrie was witness to many life-changing events happenings. She changed from a carefree girl to a woman of great depth and stamina. Written by Elaine Ulness Swenson. (344 pgs.)
$15.95 each in a 6x8-1/4" paperback.

Home Front - Read the continuing story of Carrie Amundson, whose life in North Dakota began in *Bonanza Belle*. This is the story of her family, faced with the challenges, sacrifices and hardships of World War II. Everything changed after the Pearl Harbor attack, and ordinary folk all across America, on the home front, pitched in to help in the war effort. Even years after the war's end, the effects of it are still evident in many of the men and women who were called to serve their country. Written by Elaine Ulness Swenson. (304 pgs.)
$15.95 each in a 6x8-1/4" paperback.

First The Dream- This story spans ninety years of Anna's life - from Norway to America - to finding love and losing love. She and her family experience two world wars, flu epidemics, the Great Depression, droughts and other quirks of Mother Nature and the Vietnam War. A secret that Anna has kept is fully revealed at the end of her life. Written by Elaine Ulness Swenson. (326 pgs.)
$15.95 each in a 6x8-1/4" paperback

Pay Dirt - An absorbing story reveals how a man with the courage to follow his dream found both gold and unexpected adventure and adversity in Interior Alaska, while learning that human nature can be the most unpredictable of all.
Written by Otis Hahn & Alice Vollmar. (168 pgs.)
$15.95 each in a 6x9" paperback.

Spirits of Canyon Creek *Sequel to "Pay Dirt"-* Hahn has a rich stash of true stories about his gold mining experiences. This is a continued successful collaboration of battles on floodwaters, facing bears and the discovery of gold in the Yukon. Written by Otis Hahn & Alice Vollmar. (138 pgs.)
$15.95 each in a 6x9" paperback.

Outward Anxiety - Inner Calm - Steve Crociata is known to many as the Optician to the Stars. He was diagnosed with a baffling form of cancer. The author has processed experiences in ways which uniquely benefit today's readers. We learn valuable lessons on how to cope with distress, how to marvel at God, and how to win at the game of life. Written by Steve Crociata (334 pgs.)
$19.95 each in a 6 x 9 paperback

It Really Happened Here! - Relive the days of farm-to-farm salesmen and hucksters, of ghost ships and locust plagues when you read Ethelyn Pearson's collection of strange but true tales. It captures the spirit of our ancestors in short, easy to read, colorful accounts that will have you yearning for more. Written by Ethelyn Pearson. (168 pgs.) $24.95 each in an 8-1/2x11" paperback.

Seasons With Our Lord - Original seasonal and special event poems written from the heart. Feel the mood with the tranquil color photos facing each poem. A great coffee table book or gift idea. Written by Cheryl Lebahn Hegvik. (68 pgs.)
$24.95 each in a 11x8-1/2 paperback.

Damsel in a Dress - Escape into a world of reflection and after thought with this second printing of Larson's first poetry book. It is her intention to connect people with feelings and touch the souls of people who have experienced similiar times. Lynne emphasizes the belief that everything happens for a reason. After all, with every event in life come lessons...we grow from hardships. It gives us character and it made her who she is. Written by Lynne D. Richard Larson (author of Eat, Drink & Remarry) (86 pgs.)
$12.95 each in a 5x8" paperback.

Eat, Drink & Remarry- The poetry in this book is taken from different experiences in Lynne's life and from different geographical and different emotional places. Every poem is an inspiration from someone or a direct event from their life...or from hers. Every victory and every mistake - young or old. They slowly shape and mold you into the unique person you are. Celebrate them as rough times that you were strong enough to endure. Written by Lynne D. Richard Larson (86 pgs.) $12.95 each in a 5x8" paperback.

Country-fied- Stories with a sense of humor and love for country and small town people who, like the author, grew up country-fied . . . Country-fied people grow up with a unique awareness of their dependence on the land. They live their lives with dignity, hard work, determination and the ability to laugh at themselves. Written by Elaine Babcock. (184 pgs.)
$14.95 each in a 6x9" paperback.

Charlie's Gold and Other Frontier Tales - Kamron's first collection of short stories gives you adventure tales about men and women of the west, made up of cowboys, Indians, and settlers. Written by Kent Kamron.
(174 pgs.) $15.95 each in a 6x9" paperback.

A Time For Justice - This second collection of Kamron's short stories takes off where the first volume left off, satisfying the reader's hunger for more tales of the wide prairie. Written by Kent Kamron. (182 pgs.) $16.95 each in a 6x9" paperback.

The Silk Robe - Dedicated to Shari Lynn Hunt, a wonderful woman who passed away from cancer. Mom lived her life with unfailing faith, an open loving heart and a giving spirit. She is remembered for her compassion and gentle strength. Written by Shaunna Privratsky.
$6.95 each in a 4-1/4x5-1/2"
booklet. *Complimentary notecard and envelope included.*

(Add $3.95 shipping & handling for first book,
add $2.00 for each additional book ordered.)